WHEN THE PURPLE MOUNTAIN BURNS
A Novel

Shouhua Qi

LONG RIVER PRESS
San Francisco

Long River Press
360 Swift Avenue, #48
South San Francisco, CA 94124

www.longriverpress.com
Editor: Chris Robyn
Designer: Tommy Liu

First Edition

Library of Congress Cataloging-in-Publication Data

Qi, Shouhua.
  When the Purple Mountain burns : a novel / Shouhua Qi.
    p. cm.
  ISBN 1-59265-041-4 (hardcover : alk. paper)
  1. Nanking Massacre, Nanjing, Jiangsu Sheng, China, 1937--Fiction. 2.
Sino-Japanese Conflict, 1937-1945--Fiction. 3. Nanjing (Jiangsu Sheng,
China)--Fiction. 4. China--History--1928-1937--Fiction. I. Title.
PS3617.I15W48 2005
813'.6--dc22

                              2004029157

Printed in China
10 9 8 7 6 5 4 3 2 1

To the memory of
the hundreds of thousands of souls
who suffered and perished in my hometown
during the long winter of 1937-38

To The Reader

This novel tells the story of the events that occurred in my hometown during the winter of 1937-38. Told from multiple viewpoints, it focuses on the day before the Japanese army entered Nanking (then the capital of China), and the first six days of the reign of terror that followed.

Throughout, I have relied on letters, testimonies, survivor accounts, diaries, and other documents made available through the work of many scholars, journalists, and others in China, Japan, and the United States.

A few of the main characters—John Rabe, Minnie Vautrin, Robert Wilson—are actual historical figures. The others are fictional.

My own grandfather, the most kind-hearted soul I have had the privilege to know, is the prototype of Grandpa in the novel.

The rest is my imagination.

S. Qi

His hand that yet remains upon her breast—
  Rude ram, to batter such an ivory wall—
May feel her heart, poor citizen, distressed,
  Wounding itself to death, rise up and fall,
Beating her bulk, that his hand shakes withal.
  This moves in him more rage and lesser pity
  To make the breach and enter this sweet city.

Shakespeare: "The Rape of Lucrece"

The student Fan Chi asked the Master what "ren" (humanness) means. "To love fellow humans," Confucius replied.

The Analects

Contents

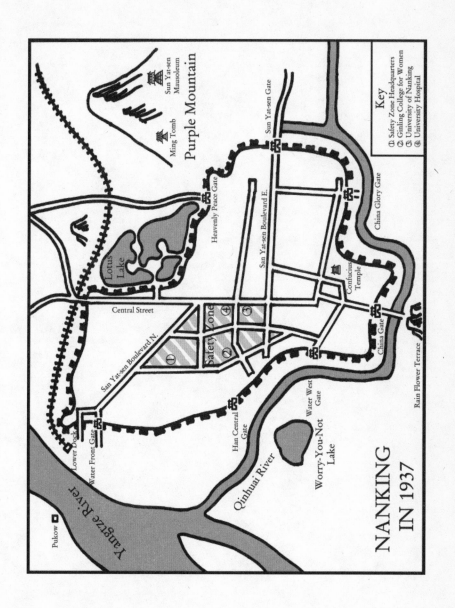

NANKING
IN 1937

Yangtze River

Pukow

Lower Dock
Water Front Gate
San Yat-sen Boulevard N.
Central Street

Lotus
Lake

Purple Mountain

Ming Tomb

Sun Yat-sen
Mausoleum

Heavenly Peace Gate

Sun Yat-sen Gate

San Yat-sen Boulevard E.

China Glory Gate

Confucius
Temple

China Gate

Rain Flower Terrace

Water West
Gate

Worry-You-Not
Lake

Qinhuai River

Han Central
Gate

Safety Zone

Key

① Safety Zone Headquarters
② Ginling College for Women
③ University of Nanking
④ University Hospital

Prologue

On August 1, 1894, the Empire of Japan declared war on China over Korean conflicts. The war lasted until April 1895 when China ceded Taiwan, the Pescadores and the Liaodong Peninsula.

On September 18, 1931, Japan invaded Manchuria, the northeastern provinces of China, and installed the puppet state known as Manchukuo.

On July 7, 1937, Japanese troops instigated the Marco Polo Bridge incident in Wanping, a city southwest of Peking; an all-out invasion of China soon followed.

By July 30, 1937, Japanese troops had occupied Peking and Tientsin.

On August 13, 1937, the Imperial Army's Shanghai Expeditionary Force landed on the south bank of the Yangtze River. Shanghai fell three months later.

By December 11, 1937, six divisions of the Central China Expeditionary Force, commanded by General Matsui Iwane, and supported by hundreds of warplanes, tanks, and battleships, had advanced to the city walls of Nanking.

They had launched massive, fierce assaults on the city from air, land, and sea—the southward bend of the Yangtze River outside the western sections of the city walls—cut off all escape routes, and the Rising Sun could be seen flapping in the gusty wind on the high points in the immediate outskirts of the city: Sun Roost Mountain in the northeast, Green Dragon Mountain in the east, and Heavenly Seal Mountain in the southeast.

Through the morning haze on December 12, 1937, from the 1,314 feet summit of the Purple Mountain in the east, front-line units of the Japanese Imperial Army could see Nanking spread out before them, ready to be taken.

Nanking (or Nanjing, meaning the Southern Capital in Chinese), founded during the reign of Qin Shi Huangdi, the First Emperor of China (221-206 BC), is approximately the size of Manhattan Island. It has been the capital city of ten dynasties and rulers, from Sun Quan of the Three Kingdoms (222-280) to the Nationalist Government of Dr. Sun Yat-sen (1912), and later Chiang Kai-shek (1927-37, 1945-49).

The city walls, built and rebuilt for defensive purposes through long periods of war and prosperity, took their current shape during the reign of the Hongwu Emperor (1368-1399), founder of the Ming Dynasty. The walls are about 20 miles in circumference and range between 40 and 70 feet in height.

The city has 13 gates, the better known of which are Sun Yat-sen Gate and Heavenly Peace Gate in the east, Water Front Gate in the northwest, Han Central Gate and Water West Gate in the west, and China Gate and China Glory Gate in the south.

Nanking is surrounded by more than a dozen mountains of various heights. The most famed among these is the majestic Purple Mountain right outside of the easterly Sun Yat-sen and Heavenly Peace Gates. In the city's immediate outskirts are the hallowed mausoleums of the Hongwu Emperor, Dr. Sun Yat-sen, and numerous Buddhist temples.

At the feet of the northeastern sections of the wall lies the azure Lotus Lake, its five islets covered with rare trees, blossoming flowers, green grass, and alive with birds year-round. Nestling outside the western sections of the city walls is the Worry-You-Not Lake with its exquisite mid-lake and lake front pavilions. A tributary of the legendary Qinhuai River flows into the city, for centuries its banks bustling with eateries, hotels, art and antique shops, pleasure boats filled with singsong girls, and poets; its air quivering with titillating fragrances, night and day, rain or shine, oblivious to the bewildered gaze of the sacred Temple of Confucius.

At the time of this story, the city had a population of around one million. It boasted ten colleges and universities (of which Ginling College for Women and the University of Nanking, both founded by American missionaries, were the best known), hundreds of secondary and elementary schools, temples, churches, and mosques, and numerous business offices, marketplaces, and foreign embassies.

The main arteries of transportation were Sun Yat-sen Boulevard, which ran through the heart of the city and connected Water Front Gate at the northeastern tip with the southernmost China Gate, and Sun Yat-sen Boulevard East and Han Central Boulevard, which linked the eastern and western parts of the city.

Modern and ancient, Chinese and foreign, old and new, rich and poor, beautiful and ignoble, one and all, had been living side by side, jostling along uneasily.

On the morning of Dec 12, 1937, hundreds of thousands of

civilians and soldiers who had not evacuated were trapped inside the city walls. All the gates were closed.

Sunday

December 12, 1937

1.

She looked outside the main room window again from her home on the second floor of a small, old building in a narrow alley.

Looking through clusters of tiny, reddish plum blossom buds from the prune tree which stood in the yard, she could see a section of Sun Yat-sen Boulevard North in the distance. The view would have been blocked if it had not been for an opening between two crumbled buildings, like a gap between two front teeth.

She had been standing by the window for hours on end during the last several days, watching flames going up the Purple Mountain, watching streams of rickshaws, squeaky donkey-drawn carts, overloaded automobiles honking incessantly, men dragging oversized trunks and suitcases behind them, porters burdened with huge bundles bobbing from carrying poles, mothers with crying babies, small children leading half-blind grandparents, soldiers in dirty, ragged uniforms, their mangled faces or arms in blood-stained bandages—a roiling human torrent of uncertainty and fear.

Every now and then sirens would awaken and pierce the air, and before bombs fell from warplanes with the Rising Sun on their wings, people ran for cover like panic-stricken rabbits, tripping over fallen bodies, screaming for their very lives.

It was a week ago when a bomb fell onto the corner eatery, claiming the lives of Uncle Liu's family and wounding several others. When she crawled out from under Grandpa's bed after the bombers had flown past, she saw a gaping hole in the thin window glass, an expansive circle of jagged shards. She applied a sheet of Grandpa's delicate, white rice paper to cover up the broken window.

Bombs had been falling from the sky since August, reducing untold numbers of homes into naked, tottering walls, and blasting newborn babies into orphanhood at their mothers' bosoms.

This morning, however, it seemed eerily quiet. The boulevard was virtually deserted. The human flood had trickled down to an occasional bicycle and a hurried pedestrian now and then.

Ning-ning turned her gaze into the distance.

The sun was about to burst forth from behind Purple Mountain, its fiery rays dispersing the early morning mist which clung to the mountain's slopes, slowly turning the sky into a blazing, scarlet red. The mountain looked less majestic than she had remembered it to be even yesterday. A few flames could still be seen, while smoke curled upward in the morning air.

A cough came from the room where Grandpa lay. Ning-ning closed the window and turned to walk across the main room toward his room.

Eyes closed, his silvery head swinging slightly to punctuate the cadence of his morning ritual, the beads of the rosary filing through his quivering fingers, Grandpa was lost in another world. The cotton-padded coat, which was supposed to be spread across his chest to ward off the cold, had fallen to the floor.

Hearing her footsteps, Larkie, in the bamboo cage on the

nightstand, hopped about excitedly.

Resting against the edge of Grandpa's bed, Ning-ning took the coat and spread it gently across his chest. Grandpa stopped murmuring, released the rosary, and took her hands in his own.

"Grandpa, you're not very warm," she said.

"I'm all right," replied Grandpa, but she could hear a faint wheezing in his voice.

Grandpa had been bedridden for almost three months now. It had happened all of a sudden. One August afternoon, she came back from a visit to Eva's school at Ginling College for Women and found him sprawled on the floor, saliva dripping from his mouth. Suspecting the worst, she screamed and ran downstairs to get help. Auntie Huang, the landlady, hurried up, put her hand close to his nostrils, and felt his pulse.

"Grandpa is still alive!" she pronounced. "I'll go and get a doctor."

With the help of Auntie Huang and other kind neighbors, Ning-ning had managed to be an effective little nurse for Grandpa. After weeks of being spoon-fed dark brown herb juices and having long, sharp needles inserted all over his body, Grandpa didn't become completely paralyzed. But he couldn't do the things he used to enjoy doing any more: practicing brushwork at the dining table with a pot of freshly-brewed green tea within reach; going to his favorite shrine to burn incense and offer a sacrifice, and especially taking Ning-ning to the market near the Temple of Confucius to see exotic birds and precious Rain Flower stones.

Incontestable evidence of Grandpa's illness was the presence of a long, rectangular, ominously black wooden box wedged between the lower end of his bed and the wall.

A coffin.

The ugliest, most hideous thing she had ever seen.

It had taken six neighbors to carry it up the narrow stairway and place it in his small bedroom. Grandpa wanted to be prepared.

Ning-ning couldn't connect that thing with Grandpa. She couldn't picture Grandpa lying in it, being carried away and buried deep underground somewhere. She couldn't imagine not seeing his kind face and hearing his tremulous chanting again.

"Are you hungry, Grandpa?" she asked.

"No," soon followed by, "a little."

"I'll go and make breakfast."

As Ning-ning turned, Larkie hopped about in the cage again.

"Trying to catch my attention?"

She stopped. Larkie cocked his little head to one side, fixed his gaze on her, his beady eyes reflecting a curious, childlike expectancy.

"Sing me a song, kiddo," she said, bending closer to Larkie, "and I'll feed you first. Promise."

Larkie cocked his head again, flapped his wings a few times, and crooned. His voice was high, rich, and melodious.

"Isn't he something, Grandpa?" she giggled.

"Yes, he's quite a singer." Grandpa's face beamed.

Ning-ning went to the kitchen, removed the lid on a vat in the corner, took a teaspoon of rice, and returned to Grandpa's room. Larkie hopped and twittered when she dropped the rice into a small wooden saucer inside the cage. Grandpa turned to watch Larkie pecking at the rice in the saucer.

Water and electricity had been shut off since yesterday. Luckily, she had saved two vats of water in the kitchen. It would last for a week or two if they used it wisely.

She lifted the pot from the stove and noticed a faint red glow inside the hole she had made in the middle of the charcoal brick. The coal was still live. Squatting, she picked up a small metal bar, slid open the vent door near the bottom of the stove, and worked to shake down the dead cinders. A gust of dry, dusty air swept over her face when she stood up to add a few pieces of new coal into the stove. She coughed.

"Are you all right?" Grandpa called out from his room.

"Yeah," she said, wiping her eyes and nose with her sleeve.

She poured a handful of rice into a bowl, washed it once, poured it into another small metal pot, added hot water to the pot, and placed it on the stove.

Soon, the pot began to hum.

She sprinkled a pinch of salt into a cup of water and rinsed her mouth, then splashed some more water on her face. After that, she walked into her parents' room to get her mother's mirror and comb. Their bedroom occupied about two thirds of the interior room and was separated from her own by a wall of thin boards and a door. They hadn't slept in it for so long. When would they be coming back?

She placed the mirror on the window sill and began to fix her hair. She remembered again how Mama used to take pleasure in combing her long, shiny hair, weaving it into two fine braids with her nimble fingers, and finishing it off with a pink or purple butterfly knot on top of her head. Whenever Mama went to visit Papa, wherever he happened to be, Grandpa would have to fix her hair in the morning, but he could not do it nearly as good as Mama. How many years had it been? Now that Ningning was older, she had done her own hair, even when Mama was home.

Ning-ning looked at the girl in the mirror. She had large eyes sparkling under long eyelashes. Her nose was small but straight, and her lips and mouth were clear. The little scar on her forehead was barely visible unless looked at closely. She smiled, pouted, and made a face at the girl.

"Vanity is vice," she said, mimicking Grandpa's stern voice and pointing a finger at the girl's nose.

A hissing noise came from the kitchen. She lifted the pot lid just in time to prevent it from spilling over. Inside the pot, a thin, creamy rice congee was beginning to take shape. She moved the vent door three quarters down.

For breakfast, Ning-ning used to walk to the corner eatery and buy a big bowl of tender bean curd pudding for her and Grandpa from Uncle Liu, who would garnish it with a spoonful of some spicy sauce to make it tasty. Now, the Liu's were gone and the eatery was nothing but a few tottering walls.

"Ning-ning," Grandpa called.

"Coming," she hurried to Grandpa's room. "You want to get up? Breakfast will be ready in a minute."

"Okay."

"Put your hand on my shoulder, like before," she instructed. Grandpa removed his jacket and the quilt underneath and began to move his legs to the edge of the bed. Ning-ning could feel the weight of his trembling hand on her shoulder, her right hand supporting Grandpa's back, her left hand guiding his long, weak legs to the pair of cotton-padded shoes on the floor. A few pains-taking moments later, Grandpa was on his feet. He gasped for air.

"Are you all right, Grandpa?" she asked.

When they finally sat down to eat in the main room,

Grandpa's bowl of congee and his spoon trembled in his hands. He had to go slowly so that the spoon would not miss his mouth.

"Grandpa," Ning-ning giggled, "you've got rice on your moustache."

"Really?" Grandpa put down the spoon and tried to brush off the sticky rice with his fingers, but he only made it into a bigger mess.

"Let me get it for you, Grandpa," she laughed.

"Grandpa's getting useless now," he sighed while she cleaned his moustache with a towel.

"You're not!" Ning-ning said when she finished. "See how good you look this morning."

She turned to reach for the mirror on the windowsill.

"No," he protested, "Grandpa has no use for that any more."

"Okay," Ning-ning said as they continued to eat, "but you really look great this morning."

"Trying to make me feel better, aren't you?"

"I can swear to—"

"No!" Grandpa coughed, his face wrinkled.

"No talking while eating, or you'll choke." Ning-ning hurried to Grandpa's side and patted him in the back. "Better?"

Grandpa shook his head, still coughing. "You should have gone."

"Where?"

To the Lower Pass Dock. That would have meant getting on a ship that would take her to Papa's folks or even some distant relatives, but Grandpa didn't like the idea of a 12-year-old girl traveling by herself.

"Go with Eva," Grandpa had said when her best friend came and told them about the Safety Zone established by a few foreigners in Nanking.

Ning-ning had shaken her head.

"Go with Auntie Huang, then!" Grandpa had urged when the landlady came up the day before yesterday and offered to take Ning-ning with her.

Ning-ning had refused.

"Why are you so stubborn?" It was the first time she had seen Grandpa lose his temper in such a way.

"I don't want to leave you behind, alone here!" She said as she stormed out of Grandpa's room.

"Don't you worry, Grandpa," Ning-ning said when Grandpa finally stopped coughing. "The Japanese will be too busy to worry about a little kid like me."

Grandpa sighed and shook his head one last time. "You're still a kid, indeed."

"See how quiet it is this morning?" Ning-ning said, looking up from her bowl.

"I hope it'll be so for a while," Grandpa mumbled, chewing slowly.

Muffled sound of explosions rumbled in the distance.

Machine-guns rattled.

Ning-ning jumped up from her stool and opened the window.

The sound became louder, closer. The floor under her feet quivered; so did the bowls and spoons on the dining table.

"It's from Purple Mountain!" she reported. "And from the south, too!"

When she closed the window, the glass shards and rice paper cover buzzed together uneasily in the wind.

"They must be pounding those gates very hard today,"

mumbled Grandpa.

She sat down next to Grandpa, putting her hands in his. Grandpa seemed to be shaking.

If only Mama and Papa were home now. They would know what to do.

It was in July when Mama was leaving for Shanghai, and she had wanted to take Ning-ning with her. Ning-ning hadn't seen Papa for almost a year by then. And it was summer recess, after all. However, with the imminent Japanese attack on Shanghai so much on peoples' minds, Mama had decided against the idea at the last minute. It would be safer to leave Ning-ning with Grandpa in Nanking, she said.

"Ning-ning," murmured Grandpa.

"Yes?"

"Are you scared?"

"No." But she knew she was. At the very least she was worried.

"Good. Now, listen, we need to be prepared."

"How?"

"First, food and water."

"We've saved up some water and that bag of steamed buns you told me to buy a few days ago."

"Good."

"We've also a bit of rice crust and some leftover rice I cooked last night."

Grandpa nodded. "Now, go and gather all the food we have in a box. We need to hide it."

"Why?" She knew the answer, of course.

Ning-ning went to the kitchen and busied herself there. When she came back with an old carton filled with all the food she had found, she could feel moisture on the tip of her nose.

"Where should I hide it?" she asked, feeling the weight in her arms. "Mama's room?"

"No, my room."

"Your room? It's so bare and—"

"That's exactly why. Underneath my bed. Nobody would look there."

She carried the carton to Grandpa's room, crawled under his bed, and pushed it to the furthermost, darkest corner. Larkie hopped about in the cage when she re-emerged from under the bed.

"It'll be all right," she bent nearer to the bird. "Promise."

Another round of explosions and machine-gun fire in the distance.

Larkie tilted his head, his shiny, beady eyes looking into her own, as if somewhat skeptical of her ability to prophesize.

"It'll all be quiet again soon, kiddo," she reassured.

Grandpa was chanting at the dining table, eyes closed, when she returned.

"Now, go get your mirror and scissors."

"Huh? Why?"

"Your hair."

She had seen young women and girls wearing short hair. Eva's hair was short, just long enough to cover her earlobes. Most of the Ginling College students wore their hair short, too. With ear-length hair, dressed in their white blouses and black skirts, these girls looked so modern.

"Give me the scissors," Grandpa said when she came back from her room.

She moved her stool closer to Grandpa and sat down.

Grandpa held a lock of her hair in his quivering fingers.

"You know what, Grandpa? Let me do it myself." She stood up and took the scissors from Grandpa. "Haven't I done a good job trimming your moustache?"

When she gripped a lock of hair from the back of her head and aimed the tips of the scissors at it, Ning-ning felt a lump in her throat. She hesitated, then began to cut.

"Give it to me!" Grandpa said when she was about to throw the first cut on the floor.

"Grandpa!" She giggled.

"Yes!"

"Okay." She placed the hair in Grandpa's hand. He looked so happy.

Ning-ning began to apply the scissors all over her head, paused now and then to check herself in the mirror. Messier than a sparrow's nest turned inside out by some mischievous boy. Papa and Mama, Auntie Huang, the twins, Eva, just about all her school friends, would have to laugh their teeth off when they saw her. Mama would probably cry, too.

Ning-ning felt sourness rushing up her nose.

"It'll grow back… " Grandpa murmured.

She kept her eyes on the girl in the mirror without saying a word.

"Before you know it."

"I know," she acknowledged grudgingly.

"Now, your face."

"What about it?" She was unhappy now.

"We have to."

"But why should I make myself look ugly?"

"You'll understand when you grow up."

"I'm already grown up! I cook and wash and clean and do a hundred other—"

"You're still a little girl."

"If you say so, Grandpa." She got up and began to walk in the direction of the kitchen.

"Not there." Grandpa said.

"We don't use soot?"

"No, that's too crude for my Ning-ning. Go get my writing set."

"Okay!" She spun around and practically danced toward Grandpa's room.

She came back with a brush, an ink slab, and several ink sticks. One of the ink sticks exuded such an exquisite fragrance as if all the plum blossoms on the twigs outside suddenly bloomed. It was a gift from Papa, and Grandpa had used it only once. It was too precious to use it too often, Grandpa had said.

"That one would be perfect for you, but—"

"But we're not going to use it?"

"No."

"Why?" She was disappointed. She sort of knew why, but not quite.

"How about this one?" She picked out an ink stick Grandpa had used for practicing his brushwork. It had an unpleasant smell but didn't stink like the cheap ones some of her classmates used at school.

Grandpa nodded.

She got a small cup of water, poured a small amount onto the slab, and began to gently rub the chosen ink stick against the slab in a circular motion.

She had never worn any makeup before.

"You're too young for it," Mama had said one morning about a year ago when she stood by the windowsill, watching Mama applying some white powder on her face.

Was she old enough now? Perhaps still too young, Mama would say, but old enough to have to wear a different kind of makeup now, for a very different purpose.

Grandpa started with her left eye. The tip of the shivery brush moved around the eyelids slowly. It had a cool, ticklish feel. She giggled.

"Sit still," Grandpa commanded. She could hear the wheezing sound in Grandpa's breathing.

When Grandpa had finished around her eyes, nose, and mouth, Ning-ning wanted to have a look in the mirror.

"We're not through yet." Grandpa sounded annoyed.

"Just a quick look."

She looked like the Monkey King in Peking Opera. If only she could be the Monkey King. She would just pull out a tiny, needle-like stick from her ear, say some magic word, and it would grow into an enormous, thousand-jin pole instantly; she would wield it and charge headlong into the enemy, whoever they happened to be, and they would all fall on their knees, prostrate themselves before her, and beg for their lives.

Or, she could pluck a single hair from her head, give it one gentle puff of air, and an army of baby Monkey Kings would leap from her open palm, waving their little magic weapons, and chase the enemy away.

Or, short of both, she could at least draw a big circle with the magic pole and create a Safety Zone of her own. She would invite just about everybody she knew to come in. All the good people, of course. No bad people, and not even bombs dropped from the sky, could hurt anybody inside the circle. Wouldn't that be nice?

A tremendous explosion rumbled in the distance.

Machine-guns crackled.

The window glass and rice paper buzzed.

"Let's finish it quick." Grandpa's brush danced across her face.

It was all covered in ink now. She could picture what she looked like without the mirror. There was no time for that anyway. Finally, Grandpa put the brush down.

"One last thing, Ning-ning."

"We're not through?"

"Not yet. A place to hide."

"Under your bed again?"

"No."

"Mama's room? Mama's closet is big."

"That's the last place you want to hide."

"Where then?"

"My room."

Grandpa's room? If not under his bed, where else?

That ugly, hideous thing in the corner?

"Oh no! Grandpa!"

"Yes." There was firmness in his gentle voice.

"You're not kidding?" She almost laughed.

"No."

"Grandpa!" It'd be so dark in there. There'd be no air for her to breathe. She'd be scared to death before being killed by anyone. She was too young to be buried alive in that ugly, hideous thing. Besides, it was for Grandpa.

"Yes," Grandpa sighed. "Nobody would look in there."

"What about..." she hesitated.

"With things going on like this," Grandpa murmured, "I may not need it after all."

"Oh, stop it, Grandpa!" She was surprised when her eyes suddenly welled up.

"End of discussion." Grandpa struggled to stand up. She gave him her shoulder right away.

They were beside the coffin now.

Ning-ning felt a knot tightening in her stomach. She had never liked the sight of the coffin in Grandpa's room, but now she had to lie inside it if she didn't want to upset Grandpa and if she wanted to get through it all.

She tried to open the coffin. Its long, bulky lid was incredible heavy. She managed by gripping its narrow edges as tightly as she could and pushing and lifting until her fingers hurt.

A strong smell of fragrant, fresh wood greeted her nose. No paint inside, just bare, yellowish planks. The heads of those black nails, still visible in the planks, looked intrusive.

"What should I do? Just jump in?"

"No, we—you need to drill a hole for some air."

"That'll ruin it!"

"Well," Grandpa chuckled, "I'd need to breathe, too...if I get to sleep in it at all, right?"

"Oh, please, Grandpa!" She giggled, too, nervously.

"Use the scissors," Grandpa instructed. "Wrap a towel around your hand, though."

She climbed over gingerly with the scissors in hand and fell flat inside the coffin.

"Be careful!" Grandpa warned, but he was too late. The

pointed tips of the scissors barely missed her face. Yes, she needed to be careful, she warned herself.

Ning-ning lay down and moved her arms and legs tentatively. A bit of room to spare all around. Not bad.

"How do I look, Grandpa?"

Grandpa didn't reply, of course.

"It's nice down here, really," she reassured.

She sat up and began to work at a spot on the floor of the coffin.

"Good, nobody will see it in there," Grandpa sounded more cheerful. "Apply pressure evenly."

She didn't make much headway at first. After turning the scissors left and right a few more times, the wood began to crackle and splinter.

"Some cheap willow," Grandpa murmured.

Before long Ning-ning had completed one hole. She could put her index finger through it.

"One more in there and two on the side and you'll be fine."

When she was finally finished, Ning-ning was exhausted. The muscles in her arms were sore and her wrists hurt. Her fingers had frozen into the shape of gripping the scissors. She could feel heat fomenting inside the cotton-padded winter coat she had on.

"Very good," Grandpa coughed, wheezing loudly.

"Grandpa, you need to get back to your bed," she said, climbing out of the coffin.

Grandpa moved to the nightstand, where Larkie flapped his wings and crooned. Grandpa reached out to touch the cage with his quivering fingers.

"Let Larkie go," he murmured. "He's been with us long

enough."

"Grandpa?"

Grandpa nodded.

"Come with me, kiddo," Ning-ning said, taking the cage from Grandpa.

She opened the window in the main room and slid open the door to the cage. Larkie cocked his head this way and that, his beady eyes gazing at her curiously.

"Yes, you're free to go," she said.

Larkie hopped to the opening of the cage, flapped his wings a few times, and leapt into the air. He flew to the prune tree and perched on a young branch which bounced a little under his weight. A few high, melodious notes came from his throat as he turned to look at her one more time, took off, and soared into the sky.

Another explosion sounded in the distance.

Startled, Ning-ning abruptly shut the window. She hurried back to help Grandpa get into his bed.

"Grandpa?" She now stood by the coffin and gazed at its interior blankly.

"Yes?"

"Have you ever seen a Japanese?"

"Yes."

"What do they look like?"

"Like us."

"Really?" She turned to look at Grandpa. He nodded.

"Exactly?"

Grandpa hesitated, and nodded again.

2.

Nakamoto Tateo was seething with rage this morning.

It was a tingling sensation and the first thing he had been aware of in the cold bed only a couple of hours ago.

Now, as he gazed toward Nanking's China Gate through the morning haze, the tingling sensation he felt gave way to a sense of urgency, and he could feel and hear his breathing quicken.

Nakamoto was smartly dressed in a thick wool uniform, his white-gloved left hand resting on the handle of the Sadamitsu at his hip, an ornamental sword made at the beginning of the reign of the Showa Emperor and bequeathed to him by *okaa-san* (Mama). He could feel the muscles of the strong-limbed mare underneath him twitch spasmodically as she exhaled steamily in the fresh morning air. A sudden flash from the rising sun struck his tall figure—he had to look tall sitting astride the grand mare— and the right side of his face glowed with a ticklish warmth.

Nakamoto wondered how he looked to Lieutenant Colonel Tajima, standing only a few meters to his left, also gazing toward the China Gate intently, and to Zenba, his orderly, who stood directly behind. If Imai Yoshio or any other correspondent happened to be present, he could take a snapshot of Nakamoto in silhouette, facing the wall. Such a picture would certainly complement a headline in the *Asahi Shimbun*, *Asahi Graph*, or any other major newspaper back home:

BRIG. GEN. NAKAMOTO TATEO
POISED TO TAKE NANKING!

He knew that at this moment his brigade was only one of many that had besieged the city and were ready to go in for the final kill. Nevertheless, toying with the idea of the picture and headline had relaxed him. He breathed more easily.

"General," said Tajima, "once the engineering unit gets its job done, we'll be ready to move in."

Nakamoto nodded.

He had selected the best of his troops, Tajima Masanori's battalion, for what would be this decisive, final assault. Although thin and small in stature, Tajima had proved to be the most dependable among Nakamoto's battalion commanders. His soldiers had been hardened by battles fought from Shanghai all the way to Nanking.

Nakamoto felt his rage simmer. Its source was no mystery.

Last night the brigadier general had enjoyed a feast of steamed pork rolls, sautéed chicken, stir-fried cabbage, and homemade rice wine. His staff had collected these from units which had been requisitioning on the side while chasing retreating Chinese troops and hunting down straggling soldiers in the surrounding area. After the feast, he stretched out in a cushioned chair, sipped sake, and watched his staff break into spirited singing. Affected by the joyous mood, he hummed along now and then and his staff sang all the more cheerfully.

What had ruined an otherwise perfect evening?

When he finally turned in, he tossed and turned in the cold bed most of the night.

He didn't get a good night's sleep because he missed his long bath.

He didn't get a long bath because even the biggest house of the village, the brick-walled, tile-roofed, multiple-room residence abandoned by a rich landowner, was not equipped with a bathing facility.

After a frantic search inside the house, Zenba, his orderly, found a wooden bathtub filled with dirty clothes in the yard outside.

The Chinese were such useless, filthy people. Their land was vast, a hundred times bigger than that of Japan, perhaps, and a thousand times richer in natural resources, but what had they done with it all? Why didn't they at least have a decent bathing facility installed in their residence? Did they ever bathe at all?

When he finally stripped himself in the main bedroom and sat in the wooden bathtub Zenba had washed clean, Nakamoto bathed gingerly, cautiously.

The water in the pond in front of the house looked harmless enough, but who knew whether or not it was contaminated? All Zenba could do was bring the water to a boil, and even then he still could not trust it completely.

Nakamoto felt filthy, irritably filthy this morning.

He felt his skin had crusted with the dust and sweat of the day.

"Zenba!" the brigadier general barked.

"Yes, general!" the orderly replied from behind.

"If you can't get me a decent bath today, I'll have you skinned!"

"Yes, general!"

Nakamoto could hear machine-guns chattering along Purple Mountain to the northeast.

Sporadic but fierce skirmishes had been occurring along various parts of the mountain, he had been told. General Matsui Iwane had issued an order not to destroy the sacred grounds of the Ming mausoleums because it would reflect poorly on the imperial glory of Japan. Even the mausoleum of Dr. Sun Yat-sen, built only about ten years ago, would be spared. As a result, use of heavy artillery in that region had been limited.

He understood the commander-in-chief of the Central China Expeditionary Force, yet couldn't help wondering what he, Nakamoto, would have done if it had been up to him. Would he have preferred the use of heavier firepower? In a heartbeat! A quicker victory and considerably less Japanese casualties. Another wonderful headline in the making.

The desire came back again, furiously. He wanted a long, delicious bath NOW! And all the scented, warm memories of his adolescence:

A young Nakamoto has arrived early on a hot summer afternoon to vacation for a week with his auntie's family, who lives on a serene, outlying peninsula in Nagasaki prefecture. He is exhausted and drenched in sweat. Auntie arranges for him to take a bath to help recover from the long hours of journeying through rugged, hilly terrain on foot.

He soaks in the huge tub filled with hot water, leans back, eyes closed, and stretches out his tired limbs luxuriously to let the water momentarily carry his body afloat.

When he finally finishes bathing, auntie shows him to his room not far from the bathroom. He dozes off almost immediately after his head hits the pillow.

The first thing he hears, upon waking up, is auntie telling Rieko, his cousin, to lower her voice. Apparently Rieko has just returned home.

"Tateo's napping."

He hears Rieko's soft voice replying in acknowledgement, and soft footfalls going in the direction of the bathroom.

Then there comes a crystal, unrushed, tinkling sound, like a little creek trickling down a pebble-filled slope...pearls dropping on to the smooth surface of a refined porcelain plate.

He feels his face catching fire instantly.

Then there is the sound of water gently splashing.

His body bursts into flame furiously.

Rieko is the prettiest thing he has ever set eyes on. Just one glance at her large, liquid eyes and her round face would set his heart racing wildly.

He knows that Rieko, whom he has dreamed about so many times before, is now naked, and is bathing in exactly the same water he bathed only moments ago. Their bodies are now intermingling in an indirect yet most intimate way.

He pictures her body, once shielded by kimonos, now revealed. He strains but the pictures are blurred, yet it is enough to send his body raging with fierce desires.

Brigadier General Nakamoto breathed audibly. A groan almost escaped his pursed lips. Turning his head to the left, he saw Tajima and the commander of the artillery unit barking orders to their troops. There was still time to continue the reverie for just a bit longer.

Nakamoto now turned his thought to the sensuous gift he had bought for himself for having survived the Ichigaya Military Academy after 6,147 hours of intense classwork and private study, a ruthless regimen of daily exercises and drills which left him like a toad stranded in a dry pond, and the yelling, pushing, and slapping in the face from sadistic officers and upperclassmen.

And for having punished himself long enough with a monk's life to purify himself. For What?

Damn! Why that hideous memory now? An inauspicious sign? No, nothing could be inauspicious at this juncture in his life. Of that he held no doubt.

What was that young geisha's name? Namiko? Yoshicho? It happened almost twenty years ago, yet he could still recall every single detail—except for her name, of course.

The young geisha is not older than fifteen, perhaps. Having taken a long, delicious bath in his room at an upscale inn, Nakamoto, a newly commissioned young officer, is sipping sake—*ginjo-shu*, his favorite kind with its rich taste—at a table, waiting.

A gentle knock sounds at his door.

She is dressed in brightly-colored kimonos. Her rich, dark hair is fixed high on her head, her moon-shaped face is rouged just right, and the dewy lips of her small mouth are like cherry blossoms.

In small, pin-toed steps the young geisha walks toward him, long eyelashes fluttering timidly over a lowered gaze. The air is dizzying with her fragrance.

A flower blooming nervously, ready to be picked.

He turns her around, shivering with urgent expectancy. Take your time (he remembered telling himself even now, so many years later), enjoy it deliberately so that you can relive every moment of it for the rest of your life. After all, being the *mizuage* patron of a young geisha will probably be a once-in-a-life-time experience for him. He wants to ensure that it will be worth every cent of the two hundred yen he has paid for the privilege.

Even now, sitting astride the mare in a faraway country, just moments before a massive assault was about to start, Nakamoto could still recall vividly the sensations he experienced when his fingers touched the cool, creamy skin of the nape of the young geisha's neck...removing her *obijime*, the cord that held the *obi*, or sashes, high between her shoulder blades...struggling clumsily with the knot (did he imagine hearing a soft, nervous giggle coming from the young geisha's throat?)...unwinding the *obi* ever so slowly...letting it fall to the floor....

The brigadier general breathed more audibly. Even the mare underneath him seemed to twitch with him in excitement. He turned to the left again. Tajima and the commander of the artillery unit were ready. The final assault would start at any moment.

Nakamoto once again trained his binoculars onto the citadel on top of the wall in front of him. Famed to be the largest ancient citadel in China, it was about 15,000 square meters in size, if the intelligence report was accurate. In addition to the gate right beneath this citadel, China Gate had three other smaller citadels, all connected by a string of four arched gates. There were also 27 caves scattered within these gates, the largest of which could hold a garrison of about a thousand soldiers.

"Tajima," he said, without turning his head.

"Sir?" Tajima stopped in the middle of a sentence to the commander of the artillery unit and turned his face toward the brigadier general on the right.

Taking China Gate will be no different from deflowering a young geisha. You'll have to peel off layers of barrier before reaching her naked self, Nakamoto thought. At the last moment he decided against sharing this analogy with his subordinate officer.

"Ready?" Nakamoto offered instead.

"Yes, sir!"

The brigadier general raised the binoculars again. He could see individual limestone blocks in the wall. So many of them looked grotesque, having been scarred by machine-gun fire and shrapnel from airborne bombs. Nevertheless, the wall still stood, the last barrier between him and what he wanted.

The forced march from Shanghai to Nanking, taking Suchou, Wuhsi, Ch'angchou, and Chenchiang along the way, was also like tearing off layer after layer of clothing. Now they had reached Nanking, the heart of China.

She would be standing—or prostrate on the ground—before him in stark nakedness in just a few short moments, ready for the taking.

Unlike a virgin geisha, however, Nakamoto knew that Nanking had been torn and pounded many times before and was covered with deep scars. He was about to inflict many more wounds and he was not going to feel sorry about it.

Why should he? How many of his brave troops had fallen while landing on the shore of Hangchou Bay to the south of Shanghai, taking Suchou, Wuhsi, Ch'angchou, Chenchiang, all the way to the high points on the outskirts of Nanking?

These damn Chinese troops. They were supposed to be poorly armed, poorly trained, lacking fighting spirit, yet they had put up such a fierce fight in Shanghai and had caused thousands of Japanese casualties. The battle there had dragged on for three months instead of being over in a week, as planned. And what about the plan to take over the whole of China in three months?

They were such untrustworthy people, too. The Chinese general, Tang, had wanted to negotiate a truce. Some tentative agreements had already been reached which would have given the Chinese troops time to withdraw while allowing the Japanese troops to march into the city peacefully. However, Tang's envoy failed to appear at noon two days ago, the deadline set by General Matsui. Now, many more of the Emperor's warriors would have to fall before victory could finally be seized.

And what about the Chinese *huaguniang*?

They were as flowerlike as Rieko, Namiko, or Yoshicho—whatever their names were, but so unsophisticated, and so uncooperative. They were not game for any fun at all. They had to spoil everything every time. Some had swooned before he even laid a finger on them. Some could not stop shaking convulsively, as if having been bitten by a snake. One, a real virginal beauty, kept sniveling so hysterically that her nasal mucus and tears had horribly soiled the *furisode*, that colorful kimono with wide, flowing sleeves; and the snow-white *shiromuku*, or bridal robe. He had thoughtfully packed a small trunkful of such kimonos before leaving Japan.

Nakamoto shook his head in disgust at the sight of the tainted kimonos. If he had flown into a range and...who could blame him?

Perhaps the *huaguniang* in Nanking would be different.

Suddenly, the ground underneath and around him trembled. Cannons and tanks roared while bombers with Rising Suns on their wings droned overhead toward the city. The mare moved uneasily beneath him.

Under the cover of intense shelling, soldiers from the engineering unit now made a dash toward the base of the wall.

Nanking should be different. How could there be any doubt? It was the capital of China, after all.

Several tremendous explosions came from the direction of the China Gate.

The sky was blotted out by thick black smoke, dust, and debris.

More earth-shattering explosions.

Machine guns barked furiously.

Tajima's—no, Nakamoto Tateo's—brave soldiers raised an exhilarating battle cry and charged forward.

A few minutes later, the smoke and dust began to dissolve. A huge rent was made in the wall, and China's biggest ancient citadel was nowhere to be seen. A lone solider was waving the Rising Sun on top of an enormous pile of smoky ruins....

"*Banzai!*" he shouted

His fellow soldiers joined in the frenzy, "*Banzai! Banzai! Banzai!*"

Nakamoto drew his sword, raised it above his head, gave the mare an impatient kick, and bolted forward.

3.

When a bomb hit the fourth, innermost citadel of the China Gate, where his regiment's command post had been stationed for the last several weeks, Colonel Ling Yao-guang was on the phone with General Tang Shen-chih, the commander of Nanking Garrison, begging for direct aerial support.

He felt a sudden wave of searing heat, a piercing ringing in his ears, and his body lifted into the air, numb, weightless, drifting waywardly before falling into a stupendous pit of darkness only a second later.

Earlier that morning, Colonel Ling had observed a large number of Japanese troops amassing less than a kilometer from the city wall, while column upon column of tanks rumbling down willow-lined country roads from the direction of Rain Flower Terrace to take their places just outside the city.

In the midst of the massive commotion in the distance, Ling spotted a Japanese commander astride a tall, ebony horse. Through his binoculars, he could see a cold, yet fiery glimmer smoldering behind a pair of gold-rimmed glasses. The small, squarish moustache between the commander's nose and tightened lips, and the shoulder strap on the wool uniform gave him away. The turtle's son must be a general.

Soon the brisk movements of Japanese troops and tanks kicked up a cloud of dust that blocked out the early morning sunshine and made the air too oppressive for Ling to breathe.

"General Tang," Ling said after reporting what he saw to the general over the phone, "today is the day Nanking stands or falls."

"You're telling me!" the general barked. "But what do you need to ensure the capital stands?"

"Aerial support, sir. Dropping a few bombs on those damn Japs would be a big help."

"You know damn well, Brother Yao-guang, I can't give you that. The Generalissimo has taken the entire air corps with him to Chunking. That was four days ago, remember?"

I'll be damned if I don't, but I need aerial support, sir! Ling swallowed whatever was on the tip of his tongue.

"And even if the entire air corps had stayed," General Tang continued, his tone tinged with a sickening sense of resignation, "that'd amount to no more than four or five squadrons, you know, and it would be no match to the Japs any way you want to play it. So, improvise the best you can."

Improvise with what? Those old, rusty anti-aircraft guns? He would be kowtowing to Lord Buddha if they could punch a few holes in the wings of Japs' warplanes.

Colonel Ling, along with a dozen other hardcore, mid-level field officers, had sat in the meeting of ranking generals and German military advisers called by the Generalissimo Chiang Kai-shek himself in mid-November to discuss the defense of the capital.

"Strategically speaking," General Li Tsung-jen, commander of the Fifth War Zone, was among the first to speak, "Nanking is a dead end. The enemy could surround it from the east, the south, and the west, while to the north the Yangtze River cuts off any possibility of retreat." He paused, then continued. "We may have some advantage in sheer numbers, but we have just suffered a major defeat in Shanghai and our firepower is far inferior to that of the Japanese. Therefore, it is my humble opinion that it would be impossible for us to fight an enemy who is enormously better armed and whose morale is at its peak right now."

General Alexander von Faulkenhausen, the chief German advisor, nodded in agreement. "We have several elite divisions under training by our capable, experienced advisors," he said slowly, eyeing everybody at the huge conference table. "These divisions can hold their own against the best of the Japanese. However, we need at least ten or twenty more such divisions and we need hundreds more well-trained, battle-hardened fighter pilots. Since we do not have these luxuries, and given the grim situation as aptly analyzed by General Li, I have serious reservations that an all-out defense of the capital would be the wisest course of action. I really wish our advisors corps had been given more time. Time. Just a few more years."

The conference room was unsettlingly quiet. Nobody else said anything for a minute or two.

That's it? Just leave the capital on a silver platter for the Japs to come and take? A disheartened Ling couldn't help wondering.

Then, General Tang Shen-chih, executive chief of the central government's Military Affairs Committee, stood up to speak.

"The enemy is approaching the nation's capital and will be at the feet of the city walls any day now. As all of you know, the capital is also the site of the Mausoleum of Dr. Sun Yat-sen, our National Father. If, when the enemy is at our door with swords, machine-guns, and bombs, all we do is pack up and run for our lives, leaving the hallowed grounds to be trampled by the enemy, how can we account for ourselves before the soul of the National Father in heaven?" General Tang paused, turned his eyes to the head of the mahogany table, then continued tremulously, "How can we ever account for ourselves before the supreme leader of our nation who has led us from victory to victory since the Northern Expeditions? I, for one, would rather defend Nanking to the last and fight the enemy to the death!"

From the corner where he was sitting, Colonel Ling saw a barely perceptible twitch in the Generalissimo's face.

Chiang himself then stood up slowly, gave his top generals and the German advisors a cursory glance before turning his gaze outside the window.

"I must concur with Brother Shen-chih," Chiang began deliberately in his thick Zhejiang accent. "We should defend the capital to the last drop of our blood! Failing this, I would have no face to meet the National Father in heaven; I would be unworthy of my ancestors, the trust that four hundred million compatriots have placed in me; my name would be crucified and spat on in perpetuity!"

The Generalissimo paused, turned his gaze back into the conference room, which had become deathly quiet.

"However," Chiang continued, "in the event that the central government has to evacuate, given the enemy's obvious superiority in firepower, who will command the defense?"

Chiang scanned the faces of the top generals, one by one. It was excruciating. Frozen in their seats, the generals kept their eyes to their notebooks on the table or whatever happened to be in the path of their vision at that moment.

How pathetic! Ling remembered thinking to himself. Where's the fighting spirit we've shown in Shanghai? Eaten by dogs?

Having made a complete tour around the table, Chiang's eyes returned to the face of General Tang and stayed there.

"Brother Shen-chih," Chiang lowered his voice, as if only the two of them were in the room.

As if a bolt of electricity shot up Tang's back, he straightened himself with a sudden, jerky movement.

"It looks like it's either you or me." Chiang let the sentence hang in midair, and sat down.

With a quivering hand, General Tang took out a white handkerchief and dabbed the sweat glistening on his forehead.

"The Generalissimo is the supreme leader of China," Tang stuttered. "The future of our nation depends on his wise leadership and personal safety. How could Shen-chih let the Generalissimo stay?"

Ling remembered thinking it rather odd. What was the Generalissimo up to? He and Tang had never been close or trusted each other. Although Tang had supported Chiang's Northern Expedition to wipe out the feudal warlords ten years ago, there had been no love lost between the two. In fact, Tang had been exiled twice from China as a result of their power struggles. Why had Chiang chosen Tang? Another one of Chiang's brilliant moves? If the defense turned out to be successful (a near impossibility, given the circumstances), Chiang would be in a position to take the credit for having appointed the right general to command the defense. If Nanking fell (a virtual certainty), Chiang would not have to shed a single tear when it came to sacrificing a convenient scapegoat.

It is wrong of you to second-guess the Generalissimo at such a time, Ling had told himself. After all, the survival of the capital, of the whole nation, for that matter, is at stake.

Thus, this morning, when bombs began to fall again on the China Gate, when the enemy's cannons and tanks roared, Colonel Ling could feel the very foundations of the city walls shake. In a moment of anger and despair, he had grasped the phone frantically and called General Tang for aerial support, even though he knew that the entire air corps was already in Chunking, which had now become the wartime capital of China.

"How about artillery support then? Any—" Ling was still shouting into the phone when he was being tossed into the air, like a lone, sun-scorched leaf caught in a gust of wind.

When he awakened, Ling felt dazed, as if, perhaps, he had already been reincarnated. His consciousness, which had deserted his body, was still falling into an icy, gaping hole. He wanted to stop falling. It was too dark, too cold down there.

"Help me," it was a familiar voice begging weakly. It was drowned out by eerie, deafening echoes all around the feathery consciousness of his former self.

"Colonel!" another voice called anxiously, "Colonel, we're getting you to the hospital!"

"The hospital?" Ling again heard the familiar voice mumbling.

"You're hurt," came the breathless reply by his side.

"Oh! Which hospital?" Hadn't all the hospitals been evacuated, too?

"The University Hospital. It may still be open." The other voice sounded familiar, too. Whose was it?

Slowly rising, the dizzied consciousness struggled to see.

Colonel Ling now felt his head pounding and discovered it was difficult to breathe. He could see a stretch of the sky, nebulous, frequented by billowing clouds of thick smoke and burnt tree branches. The world around him moaned and shook spasmodically, as if caught in waves of nausea.

The other familiar voice had come from the face of someone running alongside of his stretcher. Little Chao. The kid looked like he had just crawled back from death, his face caked with smoke and dust. He gave the colonel a toothy grin. Why did the kid stay behind? Ling could not recall.

Helen, my little girl, hasn't evacuated, either. That thought hit him hard.

"Dad," he seemed to hear Helen asking in a worried voice, "what's happened to you?"

"Why are you still in Nanking?" He had asked Helen about a week ago when he visited Ginling College. "Why haven't you gone to Ch'angsha to join your mom and little brother as I've told you so many times?"

"I'm not going anywhere," replied Helen. "Our college is in the Safety Zone. I'll be okay. Besides, I want to help Ms. Hua take care of the refugees."

Miss Hua. The American professor he had known since when?

"But you're a young woman—"

"Don't you trust me, Dad?" A hurt expression appeared on Helen's face. "I know how to take care of myself."

"You're as stubborn as—"

"As you, of course." Helen giggled, like when she was still daddy's little girl. She certainly knew how to handle her dad.

"Besides," she said, "I want to stay closer to Peng-fei."

Her husband. That young, handsome captain in the air corps. He had left Nanking with the Generalissimo, too.

"Dad," a shy smile appeared on Helen's face.

"Yes?"

"I've something to tell you."

Better be something good, he mumbled in his mind.

"You'll be grandpa soon."

"What? Me, a grandpa?" But she was still his little girl! He didn't want that to change. Not yet.

"How soon?" he asked, his eyes falling unwittingly on his daughter's belly.

"Be patient, dad. You'll have to wait for another six or seven months."

"That's still very soon. I'm too young to—" he blurted out in protest.

"Colonel?" Little Chao was running breathlessly alongside the stretcher, "you'll be okay. We're just a couple of minutes away from the hospital."

"How's everybody else?" Ling asked.

"I don't know. It's bad, Colonel, really bad. I did see Captain Wang, and a bunch of his soldiers, though. They stumbled out of the smoke right before the front citadel tumbled down."

Captain Wang Bao-zi. What a temper he had. Like a pile of dry, thorny branches under a brutal summer sun. Just a spark from a match and it'd blow up in flames. But what a damn good soldier. And the best company commander in his entire regiment.

His thoughts came back to Helen again. Why on earth had she chosen to stay? Why had he, Colonel Ling, been defending Nanking as if it were his own hometown?

It might have something to do with his first visit to the city ten years ago. He was a young second lieutenant of a triumphant Northern Expedition Army entering the famed city of Nanking. He remembered experiencing something close to a homecoming, as if he had been here in a dream, in another incarnation of his a long time before. Every street, every tree, every building, and every shop looked thrillingly familiar. Even the air had an intoxicating familiarity to it. And just hearing people talk in that open, hearty Nanking accent would stir up something deep inside him.

He found it puzzling.

Was that why even back then he had intervened angrily whenever he saw soldiers looting and stealing from the folks here?

Of course there was Helen, his little girl, who had blossomed into a fine young, modern woman here. Four years of Ginling College and the difference it had made.

Helen would be safe, he assured himself. He, too, was safe for now. Yet what would befall Nanking once the Japs poured into the city? His heart ached dully at the thought.

"We're almost—" Little Chao didn't have time to finish the sentence. An explosion nearby drowned him out.

Colonel Ling was tossed into the air again, and his consciousness, cut off from his body yet again, dived once more into a deep, black abyss.

4.

John Rabe was not happy with his breakfast this morning.

He had not been happy with his meals ever since Liang, a substitute cook, had taken over the kitchen about a month ago.

"Boy!" Rabe exclaimed at the dining table, chewing. "The ham and fried eggs taste like fish."

"Well, chicken no can help, Master," Liang peeped from inside the kitchen and replied in his delightful Shanghai Pidgin English. "Present time no got proper chow. Only got fish."

"But the butter tastes of fish, too. Do you think the cow's eating fish as well?" Rabe asked, incredulously.

"My no savvy, Master. My want to ask him."

Rabe almost spewed the food out of his mouth.

That was one of the idiotic joys he had to put up with living in China. For how long now? Almost thirty years, with only a few brief respites back in Germany. Five years more than the time he had lived in Hamburg, his hometown, and longer than anywhere else in the world combined. Wouldn't that make him a Chinese, sort of?

All but a few foreigners had left Nanking, as had the richest Chinese residents. Even the Generalissimo and his American-educated wife Mei-ling had packed up and gone about a week ago, leaving behind a city without a government, leaving behind hundreds of thousands of civilians and poorly armed troops without hope; the civilians too poor, too old, or too sick to join the exodus, the troops defending a city abandoned by the central government and the high command.

The exodus had started, half-heartedly, back in mid-August when the first wave of Japanese warplanes began their bombing runs on Nanking. The reluctant, sluggish trickle of evacuees soon developed into an earnest, maddened deluge when it was learned how ugly the battles in Shanghai had gotten. The air raids were frequent and deadly, and the Imperial Army drew ever closer to the city walls. That was when he returned from the safety of Peitaiho, the seaside summer resort north of Tientsin, where he was vacationing with Dora, the childhood sweetheart he had married in Shanghai back in 1909.

Why hadn't he left? Was it because he loved adventure so much that he would go out of his way to court oncoming danger with open arms while just about everybody else was running as far away to safety as their purse and legs could carry them?

Adventure may indeed have been in his bones. His father, a ship's captain, had filled his little son's impressionable mind with tales of the sea and the exotic ports of faraway lands he had visited. It was perhaps this restlessness in his blood that had sent him to work in Lourenco Marques, a Portuguese colony in Mozambique, not long after high school. A bout of malaria forced him to return to Hamburg a few years later, but once recovered, he set out again in 1908, this time for Peking, China.

Then, the strangest, most inexplicable thing happened. Upon setting foot in this ancient country of the Orient, Rabe seemed to have found a permanent moor: the restlessness in his blood was cured; it was as if he were home again.

Okay, he admitted, he needed to stay to protect his property, his walled residence with a lush garden, the German School he had established, and the property of the Siemens company branch in Nanking. He had been its director since 1931 after running Siemens branch offices first in Peking and then in Tientsin for a number of years. But that couldn't be all there was to it. The company didn't and wouldn't expect him to get himself killed on its behalf. He didn't have the least desire to put his life at risk for the sake of either the company's or his own property. That would be idiotic beyond the palest ray of reason or common sense.

The answer had to lie elsewhere.

He felt that the large, terrified eyes of his Chinese employees and servants, about 30 in all, including their immediate families, were on him, their "master." If he stayed, they would stay and stick to the end. Most of them were from the war-torn northern provinces. They would rather just huddle here around him because they had no home to go back to up north even if he offered them money for the trip. Many a time since September he had sat with them in the dugout in the garden and held a trembling child of theirs in each hand through the long hours of an air raid. He knew what it felt like.

The people of his host country had treated him well for three decades now. Didn't he owe them something, especially now when times were bitterly hard for them? These people didn't know where to go, and didn't have the means to flee. They could be in danger of being slaughtered in great numbers. Shouldn't he make an attempt to help them, save a few at least? These were his own people now, he concluded, weren't they? They needed him.

Yet the breakfast was really horrible.

"Liang, you'll have to do better with lunch and dinner, or—" He was cut short by loud explosions and machine-guns sputtering in the distance. The windows shook.

Rabe jumped out of his chair and hurried to the window.

Even without the heart-piercing sirens in the air, he knew that waves of Japanese warplanes would be overhead in a matter of minutes.

"Let's get to the dugouts!" Rabe shouted, grabbing the emergency bag by the dining table. It was filled with the most basic first-aid supplies. Liang, Han, his capable and trusted assistant, and the rest of his people began to hurry out of the house toward the garden.

Terrified men, women, and children were scrambling for shelter all over the garden. There were over a hundred of them.

"Calm down!" Rabe shouted. "Plenty of time!"

Either they didn't hear him or couldn't understand his German-accented Chinese. They kept running. About a dozen of them threw themselves under the flag—a 20-by-10 foot piece of canvas with a swastika painted on it. Back in mid-November Rabe had had his servants set it up facing the sky in hope of deterring Japanese bombers. So far it had worked: no bombs had hit his residence directly during the numerous air raids.

Having directed people to whatever shelter that could be found in the garden, Rabe hurried to the dugout with a sign hanging from a pole above its entrance:

SIEMENS CHINA CO. NANKING
OFFICE HOURS: FROM 9 PM. TO 11 PM.

He winked at the sign knowingly. The Siemens Board of Directors would be happy to know that their Nanking representative had shortened his day down to two hours only.

Like the other two in the garden, this dugout covered with planks and dirt was not bombproof, but it could provide protection against shrapnel. It had been designed for 12 occupants. Now more than 30 people were squeezed in it. Women with nursing babies were sitting in the middle, then women with bigger children, then men.

Huddled in a corner was a fat telegraph operator who used to elbow his way to the best middle seat every time there was an air raid, but he had been on his best behavior ever since Rabe threatened to kick him out.

His neighbor, a middle-aged cobbler, who had just sat down next to the fat telegraph operator, grinned at Rabe warmly, and mouthed "How are the new boots I made you?" Rabe gave him the thumbs-up sign.

Most of the people in the dugout were donning a crude muslin facemask, a handkerchief, or a little towel. Just in case.

Warplanes were droning overhead now. A whistle cut through the air and bombs exploded not too far away. Homes must be collapsing in flames, bodies charred and scattered. Rabe didn't need to go outside the dugout to see. He had seen it happen too many times before. He could smell it in the air.

Rabe turned to look at the small girl sitting next to him. She was shivering and the eyes in her soot-painted face were filled with fear. He took her hand and held it in his own. Another whistle split the air, followed by a deafening explosion. The ground underneath him trembled. Dirt fell all around like a brown waterfall.

He had just celebrated his 55 birthday on November 23. Among the gifts he received was a very lovely scarf, and the promise, given by a Chinese friend of Han's, of two trucks with 100 canisters of gasoline and 200 sacks of flour. Wouldn't that be marvelous! A gift like that everyday would mean that the tens of thousands of refugees camping inside the Safety Zone would not have to go hungry or shiver in the cold.

Another round of explosions thundered close by. Rabe turned to check the girl next to him again. She looked up and gave him a nervous, toothy smile.

He took out a short-wave transistor radio from his overcoat pocket. The girl next to him stared at it curiously. He turned it on.

The notes that flew from the radio were deep-toned, spellbinding; they spoke of an iron-gray, tempestuous sky, and black, silhouetted figures carrying a heavy coffin across a war-scarred landscape toward the horizon....

Beethoven's Funeral March. The second movement of "Eroica:" Symphony No. 3 in E flat, Op. 55. He knew it right away.

Absurd. Of all the music in the world....

Near the end of the program the host announced in a solemn voice:

"This music is kindly dedicated to you by the Shanghai Funeral Directors—"

The girl next to him looked frightened.

He shrugged, and turned it off before the host finished.

5.

Minnie Vautrin was making one of her daily tours again around the college's forty-acre campus.

The young mother she saw late last night still stood by the front gate, scanning the women, young girls, and little children who kept pouring in. Her cheeks were reddened by the icy cold December morning.

The woman had lost her ten-year-old daughter as they pushed through crowded streets to get to the women's college, now a refugee center for women and children. She needed to wait at the gate in case her daughter drifted past the campus. That was her hope. She had expressed it to whoever stopped to comfort her.

"Miss Hua," said Helen, who was with Minnie this morning, "Let me try again." Helen went up to the young mother and said something to her in Chinese. The young mother shook her head and remained frozen where she was, a living, human statue bespeaking the miseries of war.

Helen walked back to Minnie, shaking her head, too.

Would anyone still argue for the idiotic necessity of war? All they needed to do was to come and look at this young mother, to see the terrified women, girls, and children both inside and outside the campus, and to have a glance at what Minnie had seen at the Lower Pass Dock and train station back in late

November:

Wounded soldiers from Shanghai sprawled on the cold dirt floor in mute, convulsive agony; a soldier in rags groaning heartrendingly, gaping wounds in his nose and eyes, unbandaged, making his face a ghastly sight; another soldier with a deathlike look in his eyes, one of his legs having been blown off up to the hip, the rotting flesh in the undressed wounds emitting wafts of sickening odor....

"Miss Hua," said Helen as they walked toward the Quad in front of the Central Hall, a large building with raised eaves and imposing columns. "See the flag?"

Fluttering high in the morning breeze was a thirty-foot Stars and Stripes in the center of the Quad. Minnie had had it made back in September to signal to the Japanese bombers that Ginling College was American property. So far, Old Glory had served its purpose quite well, like the umbrella she had used all these years. It was a gift she received during her first return visit to Secor, Illinois in 1918.

"You think it'll protect us from the soldiers, too?" Minnie asked.

"Let's hope so," replied Helen.

"Somehow," Minnie said as they continued to tour the campus, "I like it better when you, or just about everybody else at the college, call me Miss Hua. It makes me feel so at home here."

"Well," Helen smiled, "it has been your home for almost twenty years now, right?"

"Yes, and if you count my early years in Anhui Province, it'll be twenty-five years."

It seemed only yesterday that a teary-eyed, ten-year-old

Minnie sat in her pew between her father and her little brother (Mother had died of sudden illness four years before), listening to a woman missionary who had just returned from China.

"Why did I go to China?" the woman cried out, her eyes glowing with passion, "because a million a month in that great land are dying without God. Can you picture what it is to die without God?...Oh, brothers and sisters, can you picture what it is to live without God? Have you ever thought of it, to have no hope for the future and none for the present?"

Bringing hope to the people of that faraway land. That would be her calling, the young girl had decided then. That was what she had been doing right after she graduated from the University of Illinois at Champaign-Urbana with a bachelor's degree in education. Now she had already celebrated her fiftieth birthday! She loved the red scrolls and the Chinese character of longevity her colleagues and students used to decorate the birthday party. She loved the birthday dinner of long-life noodles, the statue of the Goddess of Longevity they presented her, and the firecrackers they set off to celebrate the occasion. But she, already fifty years old?

Minnie sighed.

They were already on the South Hill. From here they could have a clear view of the Purple Mountain outside the city walls. The campus was filled with women and young girls with cropped hair and blackened faces. The very sight of the washings dangling on every tree branch and every shrub along sidewalks and campus walls would give any visitor a sense of the enormity of the challenge Minnie was facing: providing not only protection, but also the daily food, shelter, and the most basic sanitation for the thousands of refugees now being sheltered on the campus.

As they walked down a little path which led to a side door of the campus, Minnie stopped and frowned whenever she saw a broken shrub, a chrysanthemum stalk that had been trampled. Why can't they be just a bit more careful! She had helped in designing the campus, its magnificent Chinese-style buildings with upturned eaves and grand columns, and the well-manicured lawn alive with blossoms in spring and radiant colors in fall. She had planted many of those trees and flowers with her own hands.

"They'll grow back, Miss Hua," murmured Helen, apologetically.

"Yes," Minnie sighed. "When this madness is over, they'll all grow back and grow back fast." A pause. "I still remember the first day your dad came to school with you four years ago. Now, you've already graduated, and will become a mother soon!"

"I know! But you should have seen Dad's face when I told him. He almost fell over."

Minnie smiled.

6.

For a whole day there had never been a quiet moment.

It became much worse when artillery fire erupted again on Purple Mountain early in the evening. The skies to the south were lit up by flames, too. Grandpa would catch glimpses of a dazed Ning-ning at the main room window, her shadow being tossed against the wall by spasmodic, thunderous lightning from massive explosions. The windowpanes buzzed.

Grandpa knew that this was another storm in the sea of endless suffering witnessed by his generation. Nanking would certainly fall, and then?

Ning-ning had seemed so reluctant to tear herself away from the window.

"Grandpa," Ning-ning said, now sitting inside that hideous black box between the foot of his bed and the wall.

"Yes?"

"Be sure to wake me up tomorrow morning."

"I will." He could see a pair of eyes twinkling anxiously in a blackened face.

"Promise?"

He nodded solemnly.

Ning-ning let the lid fall back slowly and disappeared into the darkness.

He was used to suffering and wished he could bear it all

himself so that Ning-ning's young shoulders would be spared. But he wasn't one to just sit and meditate, waiting for enlightenment to strike. He was a practical, if not pragmatic Buddhist, with too much of the Confucian teachings already in his bones. He hadn't followed the Lotus or the Pure Land sutras exclusively. He read whatever was available and the ritual of daily chanting had soothed him. He hoped to reach enlightenment one day. In the meantime, he had worldly commitments to keep—commitment he could not abandon for the sake of his own afterlife. He was willing to prolong his own suffering just long enough to be there for Ning-ning. He could not comprehend her facing it alone.

"Grandpa?" Ning-ning's voice was muffled, like a voice calling from the netherworld, "You think we'll be okay?"

"Yes."

"Are you sure?"

"Yes, we'll be all right."

"Grandpa, is it because Nanking is the capital of China that the Japanese want it so badly?"

"That's right." Otherwise, why had they battered the city so hard for so long? If they could not take the jewel whole would they destroy it out of spite?

Nanking, a jewel to be sure, but a jewel with a jinx.

"Ning-ning, want to hear a story?"

"Sure, what about?"

"Nanking."

"Okay!"

Once upon a time, Grandpa began, there lived a king in central China. His ambition was to conquer the neighboring kingdoms. These kingdoms have been at war with each other for a long time. Finally, after many years of brutal battles, he succeeds and that is the beginning of a unified China.

"You mean Qin Shi Huangdi, the First Emperor?" Ning-ning asked.

"That's right."

That is over two thousand years ago. Shi Huangdi's capital is Xianyan, a city in today's Shaanxi province. He consolidates his power through reforms and repressions and is happy to see that relative peace and prosperity are settling over his land. One day, he decides to tour the new empire, to show himself as a benevolent ruler to as many of his subjects as possible.

"That wasn't too bad an idea, was it?" came Ning-ning's muffled voice.

"It was a very good idea if we wanted to keep the yellow dragon-robe and hold onto power as long as possible."

Early one morning, the gates of Xianyang, gaily-decked with colorful banners fluttering in the breeze, are thrown open. Imperial guards on strong, proud horses lead the way, followed by countless heavily-laden carts, and a huge wagon carrying Shi Huangdi himself. The First Emperor is on a long journey southward to see the rich valley of the Yangtze—the Great River, and the broad reaches of his empire bounded only by the four seas in the east.

"Oh, my!" Ning-ning enthused. He could picture her eyes widened with growing interest.

Many days later, Shi Huangdi and his long imperial caravan arrive at the north bank of the Great River, right across from where Nanking stands now. However, back then, Nanking is nothing but a cluster of small villages. The emperor is quite taken by the river's immensity, its racing currents, and the beautiful green hills and mountains in the surrounding area. Therefore, right after crossing the river, Shi Huangdi issues a decree that a city, a real city, be built right where Nanking is here today. It is called Ginling then, the Gold Mountain.

Grandpa paused to catch his breath.

Tens of thousands of laborers are summoned from the valley and other parts of the country to build a new city from ground up. While all this hustle and bustle is going on, Shi Huangdi overhears whispers that Ginling is bubbling with a sort of imperial, heavenly *qi* and that someone will be born in the city who will one day rise to become Emperor.

Disturbed, Shi Huangdi summons the *feng shui* master, credited as the one who started the rumor.

"How dare you invent and propagate such nonsense to upset the Emperor? You want your head to be separated from your body?" Shi Huangdi shouts with the fury of a dragon.

"Please, Your Imperial Majesty," the *feng shui* master prostrates in front of the throne and begs: "please cease to be angry lest it affects His Imperial Majesty's precious health. Your slave would never dare even dream of inventing anything to upset His Imperial Majesty."

"Then, explain yourself!" roars Shi Huangdi.

And here is the *feng shui* master's explanation.

Ginling is divinely favored by its location. It is nurtured by the Great River and shielded by so many enchanted hills and mountains in its vicinities.

The peak of the Heavenly Seal Mountain to its southeast thrusts so high into the misty clouds as if it were a seal bestowed by Heaven.

To its northeast towers the Purple Mountain. It looks like a crown garlanded with a radiant, purple halo from morning till night all year round.

Nestling in the environs are also the Sun Roost Mountain, the Green Dragon Mountain, and a dozen more such magnificent hills and mountains.

"Your Imperial Majesty, your slave would never dare even dream of saying one word if your slave were not convinced by Ginling's *feng shui* that someone born here will be favored by Heaven to replace the Qin one day."

Shi Huangdi is stunned.

"What would you suggest the Emperor should do to avert this disaster?" Shi Huangdi strokes his beard.

"Shi Huangdi believed the *feng shui* master?" asked Ningning.

"Did he have a choice?" Too many things had been going on in the world that couldn't be explained otherwise.

The *feng shui* master suggests bringing the water of the Huai River to the foot of the Heavenly Seal Mountain, cutting a ditch into the mountain so that the Huai River water will wash away its heavenly *qi*, and cutting another ditch through the heart of Ginling so that the water would channel away whatever *qi* that gives the place its heavenly aura; a tributary of the last ditch, a cannel of some sort, will turn westward near the city's outskirts and dump Ginling's *qi* into the Great River.

To make sure the *qi* is ruined, the *feng shui* master suggests renaming a little creek on the north side of the Purple Mountain Lock Gold Creek, meaning to lock up the golden *qi* inside the mountain.

Between cutting, locking, and other measures, the heavenly *qi* of Ginling will be sapped, the *feng shui* master promises. "That way, the Qin Dynasty and His Imperial Majesty will be secure for ten thousand years and more!"

"That's why the Huai River is called Qinhuai River today," Grandpa concluded, with a sigh.

"No wonder," Ning-ning yawned.

"Just a legend, though," he cautioned. It wouldn't be wise to believe or disbelieve such stories completely.

"I know." More yawning from Ning-ning. "Grandpa?"

"Yes?"

"Remember your promise to wake me up tomorrow morning."

"I will."

Ning-ning yawned one more time and all became quiet from her direction.

And that—Nanking being jinxed—was why...Grandpa stopped. He could hear Ning-ning's breathing becoming long and deep.

That was perhaps why, he continued to muse, all the dynasties and rulers that had chosen Nanking as their capital had been short-lived. The longest lasted 103 years, most of them, no more than a few dozen years. And the Qin Dynasty itself? It collapsed within fifteen years.

As for the Nationalist Government, the celebrations commemorating the tenth anniversary of Nanking as the capital were barely over before....

The noise outside quieted down as the night deepened. Grandpa seemed to doze, but a part of him remained awake and kept an eye on the big black box throughout the night.

7.

When the air raid was finally over, John Rabe followed the crowd out of the dugout and went to the International Safety Zone Committee headquartered at 5 Ninghai Road, the compound for the German Embassy before the ambassador and his entire staff had evacuated.

Colonel Lung from General Tang's central command came to ask Rabe and his committee to make a last attempt at establishing a three-day armistice so that the defending forces would be given time to depart before handing the city over to the Japanese.

Rabe and his committee spent the next several hours laboring over the armistice proposal, a telegram to be sent to the American ambassador asking him to help broker the armistice, a letter that General Tang had to sent to Rabe asking the committee to initiate the move for armistice, and rules of conduct for the intermediary who, under cover of a white flag, was to deliver a letter concerning armistice to the supreme commander of the Japanese troops.

General Tang wanted the armistice proposal to be worded so that no word of "surrender" would be mentioned, and that its idea would be viewed as having come from the International Committee. That way Tang would be covered and would not fear censure from the Generalissimo if things went amiss.

Want to hide behind the International Committee! What a coward! But, Rabe reminded himself, as long as it could save lives, nothing else mattered.

At around six o'clock in the evening, Colonel Lung came back and declared that the committee's efforts had been in vain. It was too late for an armistice now: the Japanese were already at the gates.

With a heavy heart, Rabe headed home. A few minutes later, he saw artillery fire erupting on the Purple Mountain again. The whole mountain and the entire northeastern sky, was in flames. He stood there and watched, dazed.

About three months ago, Rabe had taken a visiting friend of his to see Sun Yat-sen's mausoleum at the Purple Mountain. The gates were surrounded by bamboo scaffolding draped with dark cloth. The old Ming mausoleum was off limits, too. The presidential palace, which no one had actually lived in, was painted black from top to bottom. It looked like a huge, bloated coffin.

Would these hallowed grounds fall into charred ruins today? Rabe shook his head. It would be cruel to even picture that in his mind. He remembered the old saying: "When the Purple Mountain burns, Nanking is lost."

That same day in mid-September, while strolling atop the walls near the China Gate with the visiting friend, Rabe had spotted a bright red cap lying amid a clutter of wilted grass. Curious, he picked it up. A swarm of black flies exploded upward. Rabe stared in stark horror at something fleshy on the ground: it was a half-decomposed head of a child covered with fat, white maggots. He let the hat fall, just as someone else must have done.

Now, as he continued on his way home, Rabe saw large

numbers of civilians fleeing through the streets of the Safety Zone, followed by a stream of retreating soldiers who were still wearing straw sandals and thin, torn summer uniforms, their faces contorted by smoke, dust, and spasms of panic.

"What's going on?" Rabe stopped a soldier and asked.

"The Japs! The Japs are right behind us!" replied the soldier breathlessly. He had nothing but a small bundle of bedding and a dented canteen on his back.

When he reached his home on Han Gateway Road, Rabe had both his valise with the most necessary toiletries, and the medical bag with his insulin, bandages, and other first-aid supplies taken out to the dugout. What else? What else? He kept asking himself while running through the rooms.

Next to his old Underwood typewriter in his office was his swastika armband.

Almost anyone else on the International committee, Lewis Smythe and M.S. Bates of the University of Nanking, Reverend John Magee of the American Church Mission, and George Fitch of the YMCA, could be an excellent leader during these tough times. But he, John Rabe, had been chosen. His status as the deputy leader of the Nazi branch in Nanking could prove useful, they had said. For his part, Rabe didn't feel the need to be apologetic about his Nazi connection. After all, the Nationalsozialistische Deutsche Arbeiterpartei was all about the workingman and the poor, wasn't it?

He grabbed the armband and stuffed it in his overcoat pocket.

On the dresser in his bedroom Rabe saw a picture of Ursula, his five-year-old granddaughter. What a pair of eyes! And her hair! He hadn't seen her for how long now? He picked up the picture, gazed at it tenderly, then removed it from the frame, and put it in a pocket close to his heart.

Now he was ready.

By eight o'clock that evening, the southern horizon was awash in red flame. Rabe opened the front gate of his garden to let in the people huddling outside. Since there was no more room in the dugouts, he directed people to various sheds and to the corners of the house. Most had brought their bedding and lay down in the open. Two families spread their beds out under a large German flag. Rabe ran through the garden like a watchdog, moving from group to group, scolding here and calming there. In the end, with Han's assistance, he found shelter for everyone inside his garden.

Back in his house, Rabe put on his steel helmet, and pressed a helmet down on Han's head, too. They looked at each other and laughed uneasily: Two more fleeing soldiers from the southern gates?

At nine Colonel Lung came again and told Rabe in confidence that General Tang had ordered the Chinese retreat for between nine and ten that evening. As for Tang himself? The general had already broken away from his troops at eight and boarded a boat at the Lower Pass Dock for Pukou, on the other side of the Yangtze.

So Tang was gone, too. He would not be staying to live or die with Nanking, as he had once vowed. Mayor Ma, with whom Rabe and the International Committee had been working closely in establishing the Safety Zone, had left yesterday. Nobody was in charge now.

Lung was left behind to care for the wounded. He pleaded with Rabe to help and handed him 30,000 Chinese dollars. The money would be used to help those remaining in Nanking.

"I'll do my best," Rabe said, shaking the colonel's hand. His heart ached at the thought of the mute, unspeakable agonies of the wounded, unattended, without any medical help.

When finally it seemed that there wasn't anything else he could do for the day, Rabe sat down at his old typewriter to write another entry in his wartime diary. He must look rather odd, he thought: a steel helmet, thick-framed glasses, bushy moustache, binoculars dangling from the neck. Marshal John Rabe? No... John Rabe, self-appointed Mayor of Nanking... that wouldn't sound too bad. He grinned, typing away.

Around midnight he finally lay down on his bed. He had been wearing the same clothes for two days. Every joint in his body ached.

"*Gute Nacht*," he mumbled to himself.

His guests were settling in for the night as well: around 30 of them asleep in his office, three in the coal bin, eight women and children in the servant's lavatory, and the rest of them in the dugouts or out in the open, in the garden, on the cobblestones. Everywhere.

Mayor John Rabe, what do you need to take care of the thousands of refugees in the Safety Zone? He was nodding off fast. What about finances, policing, housing, sanitation and health, food... he had wanted bread and cheese for supper, but had none of that. If the ham and fried eggs taste like fish again tomorrow, it would be the last—

He sank into deep sleep before finishing the thought.

Monday

December 13, 1937
The First Day

8.

Tajima's battalion was among the first units that blasted their way through the city walls.

A couple of hours after midnight, while other units were still pounding China Glory, Sun Yat-sen, Heavenly Peace and other gates of the city, his battalion was already charging into the city, mopping up retreating Chinese troops. Even though it was still quite dark, Tajima would glance back every now and then as if he could see the Rising Sun fluttering proudly on top of where China Gate had once been.

He "saw" something else too. Bodies of thousands of soldiers of the Nagoya Division that had been mowed down while attempting a forced landing at the Wusong Dock right outside Shanghai, where the Yangtze River merged into the South China Sea. He came upon them, scorched by the late summer sun. He had put a hand to his nose instinctively: the bodies had decomposed grotesquely, the entrails bursting through ripped, parched skin, the bones cleaned by armies of maggots, the swarms of fat, black flies buzzing from one corpse to the other.

That was what met his eyes when Tajima landed at the same embankment back in late August. A hardened solider even then, Tajima was dazed and shocked by what he saw. Had they underestimated the strength of the Chinese resistance? Now, with the memory assaulting his senses as he moved forward in the predawn darkness, he again smelled the putrid stench of death, and his body trembled with blinding anger. And hate.

Since that day at the Wusong Dock, Tajima had been fighting with a fuming vengeance. By the end of three months of brutal battles, he had lost two thirds of his company, thanks to the damn good fight the Chinese had put up to defend Shanghai. When a triumphant Imperial Army at last turned to march westward to Nanking, he found himself in command of a newly reinforced battalion. He became Lieutenant Colonel Tajima Masanori.

The Japanese victory in Shanghai seemed to have dealt a fatal blow to the Chinese resistance. After Shanghai they had simply lost the will to fight. Over a stretch of more than three hundred kilometers, and at each one of the five or six important cities and towns in between Shanghai and the capital, the Chinese troops put up a half-hearted fight for a few days and then just turned around and ran. Within a month, Tajima had advanced to the city walls of Nanking.

From the fierce skirmishes Tajima's battalion had encountered in the outskirts and outlying areas, and from the intelligence briefings he received from Brigadier General Nakamoto Tateo, Tajima had been bracing for another Shanghai—a fierce resistance akin to a last stand. After all, Nanking was the capital and was being guarded by more than a dozen divisions, more than twice the number of Japanese troops.

Then, almost as if by magic, the ancient city wall was breached.

He couldn't believe it, even when he saw the gaping holes in the wall with his own eyes. Those Chinese, Tajima mused. If this were Tokyo, he and his warriors would have lived or died on the wall.

Tajima took a deep breath, his left hand caressing the handle of the sword at his hip. Up ahead he could see the tail end of Akiyama Yoshichika's company that was already spearheading into the city.

The streets were strewn with abandoned rifles, bedding, torn uniforms, and dead bodies huddled amid collapsed roofs, fallen walls, and smoldering ruins.

Outside the city, the slopes of Purple Mountain had quieted after a night of thunderous explosions. The morning air still quivered with sporadic gunshots from Tajima's own troops. The sky over the mountain began to glow with a ghostly pale light.

Tajima saw a soldier from Captain Akiyama's company running back toward him.

"Sir," the soldier reported, "a large number of Chinese troops, about half a kilometer ahead, are ready to surrender."

"How many?"

"Don't know yet, sir."

"Tell Captain Akiyama to approach cautiously, just in case."

"Yes, sir!" The soldier turned around and soon disappeared into the dim, early morning air.

An interesting development, Tajima thought, prancing ahead. In a few minutes, he saw it.

A huge white bedsheet fluttering pitiably tied to a tree. He chuckled contemptuously while picturing panicky Chinese soldiers ransacking residents' homes to find their white flag.

Then, he stopped, stunned by what he saw.

He had entered a large city square, paved with flat stones. Its periphery was barely visible in the nebulous early morning air. The square was occupied by an immense blur of human forms sitting on the ground, motionless, like animals, like ants, like worms. There must have been a thousand, a full-force regiment at least. A dozen more white flags made of white shirts dangling on raised sticks or tree twigs, the occasional twinkle of a cigarette drag near and far, giving him a vague sense of the vastness of whatever was sprawled in front of him.

They had all just surrendered, refusing to fight the enemy. But why? Because to live, even as a coward, seemed preferable than to fight the enemy to the death in the battlefields? Tajima couldn't understand that. Surrendering to the enemy? Wouldn't it be a hundred times worse than death itself? He would never consider such a shameful, despicable act under any circumstances.

His troops had already surrounded the large square, machine-guns had been mounted, and bayonets drawn toward the sitting human forms. Tajima realized that he had thousands of prisoners on his hands now, soldiers who had apparently been abandoned by their commanding officers.

He had dealt with Prisoners before and had heard of a set of top-secret "KILL ALL CAPTIVES" orders issued recently, but the sheer size of the prisoners in front of him made killing them all a major undertaking.

Lieutenant Colonel Tajima called for the three company commanders to gather around him and gave them instructions.

Captain Akiyama then walked in front of the massive multitudes on the square.

"Listen," Akiyama shouted in his slow, broken Chinese, "you will be led to different places so that surrender procedures can be conducted properly!"

After a moment of confusion, the prisoners stood up all at

once—a frightening forest of ragged uniforms, dust-caked faces, and eyes filled with something between hope and despair.

They formed columns, five deep, each column following a white flag and a junior Japanese officer, who was barking orders all the while, and marched in twenty directions at the same time, like sheep, bayoneted rifles pointed at their backs.

Could these be the warriors that had been defending the city over the last few days? Tajima wondered as he followed the long, thick column closest to him toward open ground not far from the square.

The platoon leader, a newly commissioned young officer, made the prisoners form lines of nine each. After a few confusing minutes, about twenty such lines were formed. The young officer stood in front of the prisoners awkwardly, apparently at a loss over what to do next.

It was Kuroda Senji, a cadet fresh out of the Army Infantry School, who had been assigned to Tajima's battalion right after Shanghai. The poor thing still needed some real training.

Lieutenant Colonel Tajima jumped off his horse. "I'll show you how!" he roared to Kuroda, and marched to the first line of prisoners.

During his first year in middle school, Tajima used to be pushed around by bullies as the notorious "sissy" of the class. His homeroom teacher, Mr. Sakawa, a middle-aged man with a quick temper and veins bulging on his forehead like worms, would scream at him in front of the entire class:

"You'll grow up to be a disgrace to the Empire! I'll bet you a thousand yen on that!"

Even his parents seemed to have resigned themselves to the fact that their sheepish boy would never amount to anything. If only the old rascal Sakawa, if only *otousan* (Papa) and *okaa-san* were all here now! Still thin and small in stature, Tajima had proved them all wrong. All it had taken was seeing blood in real battles and an enormous amount of mulish willpower.

Tajima stopped about a meter away from the first prisoner in the line, a lad about fifteen or sixteen years old who was shaking uncontrollably. Several prisoners behind the lad began to remove their watches or whatever they thought were valuables in their persons and raised them above their heads.

Want to bribe your executioners? Tajima thought, drawing out his Wakizashi sword. It was a family treasure that *otousan*, a veteran awarded the Order of the Rising Sun for his valor during the 1904-05 Russo-Japanese War, had bequeathed him the night before Tajima was leaving for the Army Infantry School. From then on, Father's spirit had been guarding him wherever he went.

Tajima spun the sword around a few times, its long, sharp blade glinted in the first flush of morning sunshine. He rested the back of the blade on the lad's neck to judge the distance, checked the position of his legs, turned the blade back to the front, drew it back, and in an elegant, sweeping arc, let it fall.

There was a swishing sound, like the sound of the wind stirring in the trees, and before the young lad's head hit the ground, a thick stream of blood shot forth fiercely from the neck stump. The lad's knees buckled and he fell lifeless to the ground. Tajima felt a splash of thick, warm drops on his face. There was a salty taste. He spit.

Wiping his sword with a towel, Tajima turned to glance at poor Kuroda, who was standing about two or three meters behind him, watching with apparent unease. Still further behind was the figure of Brigadier General Nakamoto astride his tall horse, silhouetted against the pale, early morning light. So the general had caught up, too.

"Come closer, young man," Tajima growled to Kuroda. "You'll learn."

As he moved on to the second man in line, a voice, somewhere in the group, broke into song. A few long seconds passed, but then all the prisoners, all of them, joined in. It was another one of those "Resist Japan" songs. Tajima had heard them before in the northeastern provinces and in the streets of Shanghai. They sang as if they accepted the inevitable fate that was to befall them.

Tajima muttered to himself. You should have been singing with your rifles, your machine-guns, and your cannons in the battlefield just a bit more fiercely. Ten hours ago, yesterday, last week. Now? Too late.

Quickly now, he raised his sword above the downturned head of the second prisoner, a disheveled fortyish man in a dirty, blue cotton-padded coat, and struck. The man's face was frozen in agony as the sword cut cleanly through his neck. His body collapsed amid a shower of red spray. His head thudded to the ground and rolled pitifully at Kuroda's feet.

Tajima progressed further along the first line of prisoners with unabated ferocity. The memory of the Wusong Dock came flooding back and animated his limbs. He felt like an authentic reincarnation of Miyamoto Musashi. He struck repeatedly. Three. Four. Five. Six. Death, certainly, was instantaneous. He was being merciful. He paused to check if his sword got bent or warped, and struck again. Seven. Eight.

He had heard of the "contest to cut down a hundred" that

had been going on between two second lieutenants. It had started two weeks ago in Ch'angchou and had been cheered along by glowing reports in the Tokyo *Nichinichi Shimbun*. By the time they reached the outskirts of Nanking, the second lieutenant from Yamaguchi prefecture had already killed 106 with his sword while the other second lieutenant's tally stood at 105. They had decided to extend their game, and only two days ago a "one hundred and fifty campaign" had begun.

Not bad, Tajima thought as he struck the ninth and last prisoner in the line. With the last swing, he felt a slight tingling and soreness in his arms. He breathed deeply. Given time and a good sword, he thought, he could perhaps surpass one hundred and fifty himself.

Nine headless, crumpled bodies now lay where the first row of prisoners once stood. The ground was covered in blood. The severed heads, eyes upturned, lay randomly where they fell or rolled.

The singing had stopped. The prisoners stood in silence, teetering on the brink of collapse, their heads hanging on their chests.

Lieutenant Colonel Tajima turned and grinned at Kuroda. He wiped the sword clean before placing it in its scabbard, marched to where Brigadier General Nakamoto was, and saluted. The general nodded.

As he and the general turned to leave, Tajima heard Kuroda barking orders to his soldiers. It will be quite a pretty sight once they have finished here, Tajima thought. Better than Wusong Dock.

Breakfast was being prepared for General Nakamoto in front

of a house a little further down the road where a small table had been set up. As Tajima joined Nakamoto he felt tired, but his spirits were high. His nostrils opened to the fragrant aroma of rice being cooked, and he felt deep pangs of hunger as his stomach twitched.

"Sir," Zenba came up to Brigadier General Nakamoto, "breakfast will be ready in a minute."

From one of the neighboring houses the men heard a muffled, but unmistakable, sobbing. A woman crying? Tajima wondered.

"I'll go and have a look, sir," Zenba said to Nakamoto and walked a few paces away to a nearby house where the roof had collapsed and the front door lay broken on the ground.

Zenba disappeared from view for only a moment before returning, "It's a *guniang*, sir," he reported with a smile, "a *huaguniang*."

Tajima laughed, "A flower-like girl here, now isn't that something?"

There was a pause, as if Tajima had waited in deference for the general. Nakamoto looked up from a trance, glanced down at his uniform, his gloved hands, and his mud-stained boots, and shook his head.

Tajima stood up slowly and proceeded to walk toward the house. As he passed Zenba, he winked almost imperceptibly, and whispered, "Our general is a bit... fastidious, you know."

He stepped inside, and saw bodies lying sprawled on the dirt floor. An old man in a dark-colored cotton coat had been cut in half at the waist. An old woman was sprawled next to him. She had been stripped from waist down, her belly smeared with agglomerated blood. Huddling in a corner of the room was the girl, who was trembling uncontrollably and nearly choking on her own sobs.

"*Guniang*," Tajima said in his broken Chinese, grabbing the girl's collar to pull her up. His hands touched the soft skin of her neck. "*Weishenme ku*?" Why do you cry?

The girl raised her head slowly with a vacant, expressionless look. Her long eyelashes were caked with dirt and dust; her tears creating rivers of black which streamed down her soot-covered face. Tajima guessed she was no more than fifteen or sixteen.

A *huaguniang*, indeed. Tajima looked her over, as a sudden lust leapt up and coursed through his body.

How could the soldiers have possibly left her untouched? She must have been hiding somewhere and just crawled out, only to discover....

Tajima threw the girl to the floor and crashed on top of her, hungrily.

9.

"Fuck!" cursed Wang Bao-zi, captain of Colonel Ling Yao-guang's third company, as he emptied his last round of ammunition into the advancing enemy.

There were simply too many of them and they came in too fast, much like the hordes of locusts Wang had failed to repel in his home village in Henan just about every summer as far back as he could remember.

Back then, Bao-zi and his folks could hear them coming as they stood at the edge of their fields: the air shuddered with a mournful drone and a dreadful, ominous urgency. Unconcerned, Bao-zi turned to pee one more time, but before the first drop hits the dry, powdery earth, the locusts are already here, thunderous, clouding out the sky, turning the world into a rasping blur of dirty yellow, and diving headlong into the thick patches of beautiful brown wheat awaiting the harvest.

Those bugs. Completely oblivious to Bao-zi and everyone else beating and crashing on drums, gongs, pots and pans. In only a few moments the dirty yellow cloud rises into the air again, and is gone, leaving behind only bare stalks, and a young Bao-zi staring at the ground agape and stupefied.

"Gou-zi, time to go!" Captain Wang shouted to the soldier in a torn uniform kneeling next to him.

Gou-zi seemed frozen there, propped against a piece of broken limestone, his right index finger rested on the trigger of his rifle. Wang saw something wet, dark, and shiny on his left temple, matted by a lock of thick black hair. Wang grabbed Gou-zi's arm and tried to pull him up, but it was dead weight, and when Wang released his grip the soldier fell over with a dull thud.

That was when Captain Wang began to run.

It was roughly six miles from China Gate at the southern tip of the city to Water Front Gate at the north. For Wang it was a trip through hell, through fallen walls, abandoned weapons, uniforms, and bodies. Mortally wounded soldiers in the throes of death, fleeing soldiers shedding their uniforms and ransacking abandoned homes for plainclothes. As he neared the Water Front Gate, Wang spotted another officer limping alongside,

"Where were you positioned?" Wang asked.

"Heavenly Peace Gate," came the breathless reply in a heavy Shangdong accent. "Didn't you hear General Tang's retreat order?"

"Shit! When was that?"

"The retreat was supposed to happen between nine and ten, but some units got wind of it early and others, like us, never heard from anybody and just kept on fighting!"

By the time he reached Water Front Gate, Captain Wang saw the remnants of the sandbagged barricades, piles of abandoned artillery, machine-guns, rifles, overturned trucks, buses, cars, horse-drawn wagons, and charred bodies of both soldiers and civilians. The gate was the last way out, but all that lay outside was the Yangtze River.

The miserable procession of humanity pouring through the gate encountered only the muddy banks of despair along the Yangtze River: abandoned tanks half driven into the water, trucks, weapons, bags, trunks, bedding and the detritus of human existence lay scattered along the riverbank as capsized boats, doors, timber, and dead bodies whirled along toward the sea.

Now, enveloped in the cold of a dark morning of a new day, Captain Wang and thousands of others were still stranded at the riverbank. There was nowhere to go. They were huddling together, shivering, and waiting.

He heard it. The sound evoked memories of the droning locusts descending on the fields of ripened wheat back in Henan.

He could feel the earth roll and rumble.

A minute later he saw the first tank, followed by a second, and then a third, tumbling toward them. Swarms of Japanese soldiers followed. Machine guns were set up on the embankment.

Before long, a tight circle of Japanese soldiers with machine guns, bayoneted rifles, and lean, wolf-like dogs had closed in around them.

They had been taken prisoners.

Unarmed, they were like thousands of stalks of wheat that had already been stripped bare. They could all be mowed down so easily now. Would it have been better to stay and die at China Gate, fighting to the end?

But Wang's desire for self-preservation was too strong. He even pictured himself as a coward, running away from his position, limping through miles of death and destruction strewn all around him. For what? So he could live a few hours longer? Wang hung his head and gasped for breath.

Across a veritable sea of heads, Wang noticed a Japanese commander on horseback barking commands to his subordinates. Wang was too far away to see the commander's face clearly, but could tell that he had a long beard. An interpreter, who seemed to be Chinese, called out in a loud, squeaky voice:

"Surrender! If you surrender, we won't kill you!"

Following the example of everybody around him, Wang turned his torn cap backward. There was no use doing anything rash now.

"You've all been liberated!" Came the voice of the interpreter. "And to show you the kindness and glory of the Emperor of Japan, we're going to release you! You can go straight home and be peasants again!"

The prisoners were told to make feeble little white flags out of whatever cloth they could find, and form a column of five or six deep, and march north along the riverfront.

I guess I won't die today after all, Wang thought as the head of the long column at last began to move. A wave of both shame and relief hit him.

By the time the people immediately around him turned to merge into the column, Wang could see a long, blurry line of prisoners zigzagging ahead between the water on the left and the embankment on the right. The figures were silhouetted against the pinkish northeasterly sky, a subdued dragon moving ahead in deep, mute humiliation.

The Yangtze River was just a few meters away from him. He could feel the Great River's deep breathing, its troubled, foamy waves splashing an icy mist on his numb face.

Where would he go after all this was over? Looking for Colonel Ling and his former units? Where would they be now? How many of the troops had actually survived? What about returning to his home in Henan to take care of his old folks and to plow the few acres of wheat fields again?

Perhaps he should get married, have a bunch of kids, and

live a quiet, ordinary life. That would make his folks brim with happiness. The prospect of leaving the world without having seen their grandkids first had worried them for so long.

He should have married Cui first. Cui. That was the girl he would have loved to marry and would have begged his folks to ask a matchmaker to make the arrangements. But he had joined the Northern Expedition army to fight the warlords. He didn't want to marry her one night and leave her the next morning. What if he got killed on the battlefield?

If Cui were still alive today, she would be the mother of several kids by now.

A quiet, ordinary life. That would be nice, but what if the Japs followed him to his home in the hinterland province? Wasn't it their ambition to take over the whole of China? Where else could he go then? He would have to take up a gun again. What other choices would he have? No one could live a quiet, ordinary life now.

Wang suddenly saw shapes moving behind the embankment. Others must have noticed, too. His body tensed. The dragon-like column began to agitate, the prisoners looked at each other and then all around, necks stretched and craning in every direction. Without warning, the ear-splitting staccato of machine-gun fire erupted upon them.

They crouched, then tried to scatter and run, but with the embankment on their right and the river on their left, there was nowhere to go. They ran in circles. The bullets rained down upon them in an unabated fury like locusts devouring a crop field. Dirt and sand were kicked into the air. Mad, desperate screams as bodies crumpled. Flashes of blood and torn flesh exploded into the air amid the chaos.

Wang broke into a run, but he had not gone more than a few steps when something hot and piercing tore into his side. He felt he could keep going but suddenly he fell to the ground.

"Fuck! FUCK!" he cursed, and dropped to his knees. People stumbled, falling on top of him. He was knocked over now, his legs crushed by bodies piling all around. He lay on his back, immobile.

The machine guns had stopped. He tried in vain to free himself but he had no strength. He could hear the desperate cries and agonizing groans of those others around him who still lived. "Fuck you! Fuck you! Fuck you!" A single rifle shot rang out. Then another. And another.

He tried to turn his head.

The big machine guns were quiet. The Japanese soldiers had descended into the carnage. Wang could see that their bayonets were dripping red as they stabbed, slashed, and hacked at anything that still moved. A Chinese soldier who lay nearby was set upon and cut open with bayonets and eviscerated, his innards flung into the air.

Wang tried to close his eyes, but he had lingered on the horrible sight too long. Now it was too late. A dirty figure in a yellow uniform ambled over toward him. "What's this? Some foot soldier!" Wang thought, "Well I'm a Captain Goddamn it!"

In an instant, he saw a brief flash of a blood covered bayonet and felt his chest pierced as if with a knife. His lungs collapsed and he struggled for air. He felt the blood lapping somewhere against the back of his throat. He tried to take one last breath but there was only a gurgling sound. After that, there was only darkness.

10.

A ray of pale sunshine filtered through the main room window.

The house continued to shudder as explosions and artillery fire echoed in the distance. When there was quiet, a faint, barely audible breathing sound came from the coffin at the foot of his bed.

Grandpa murmured to himself and resumed chanting silently, grasping the rosary moving methodically through his trembling fingers.

A faint rustling sound came from inside the coffin. He was about to warn Ning-ning to get up slowly, when instead he heard a loud thump.

"Ow!" came a muffled voice from inside.

"Are you all right?" Grandpa asked.

There was no reply.

"Ning-ning?"

"I'm okay. I hit my head against the lid!"

"I heard it. You thought you were getting up from bed like before?"

"Yes. Wasn't that stupid of me?" Ning-ning burst out laughing. The coffin lid rose slowly, paused briefly, then continued to open fully. Ning-ning's head appeared. She squinted at bit, then rubbed her forehead. There was a pained look on her face.

"It was my fault," Grandpa said regrettably.

"I should have known better," Ning-ning said, stepping out of the coffin.

"Let me see." When Ning-ning came over to his bedside, Grandpa reached out to examine her forehead with his quivering fingers, but stopped short of touching it.

"You've got some swelling there. Go and apply some cold water on the spot."

When Ning-ning came back from the kitchen, he said, "we'll have to figure out a way to avoid that happening again."

Ning-ning helped Grandpa get out of bed and walk him over to the table in the main room. He sat as she busied herself with preparing breakfast in the kitchen.

"Sorry, Grandpa," Ning-ning said, coming back to the main room. "The stove must have died. The coals...."

She stopped herself and listened. Grandpa heard it, too.

A rumbling noise, muffled at first, but it seemed to be growing more intense. The windowpanes, the cups on the table, even the ground at their feet and the air inside the house trembled with agitation.

The rumbling soon reached a crescendo as column after column of tanks plowed their way along Sun Yat-sen Boulevard North, crushing asunder the debris and discarded belongings which littered the road. Next came the marching sounds of booted troops.

Ning-ning walked to the window and placed her hand on the latch.

"Don't!" he commanded.

Ning-ning turned and gazed into his face.

"We'll have to do without a hot breakfast today." Grandpa said. There were still some cold, half-stale buns hidden under his bed. Ning-ning helped Grandpa back into bed. She then found a long-handled umbrella and, using it to prop open the coffin's lid, climbed inside and lay down.

"Remember," Grandpa instructed, "if you hear anyone coming upstairs, close the lid, gently, and stay put, no matter what happens."

"What about you, Grandpa?"

"I'll be fine."

He fingered the rosary, closed his eyes, and resumed chanting silently.

"Grandpa," Ning-ning called in a whisper.

"Yes?"

"Any Japanese soldiers coming up?"

"No."

"Grandpa, are you praying to Lord Buddha?"

"Yes."

"Is he going to help us?"

"I believe so."

"Should I pray, too? Lord Buddha might hear us better if we both pray, right?"

"Good thinking." He imagined Ning-ning praying earnestly with folded hands.

Amid the rumbling, Grandpa could hear the boards creak in the hallway outside. Someone was coming upstairs. He knew the sound without having to think about it.

"Close the lid and don't make any noise," he whispered.

"Grandpa? Grandpa?" Came a voice from outside the door.

It was a familiar sound. "Are you in there? It's me. Ning-ning! It's Auntie Huang! We came back after midnight. We could not get out through Water Front Gate. It was closed."

"Oh, it's you!" he whispered back.

"Just let us know if you need anything."

"We will. Look after yourselves and be careful."

Grandpa could hear Auntie Huang's slow, soft steps descending the stairs. The boards creaked under her feet.

"Did you hear that?"

"Yes," replied Ning-ning. "So, Da-mei, Er-mei, they're all back."

"Yes. Feeling better?"

"Mmmm."

"Ning-ning," he said.

"Grandpa?"

"Still remember the Tri-Character Scriptures I taught you?"

"I learnt that nursery rhyme ages ago!" Ning-ning began to chant:

Such are humans
Innocent when born
Similar in nature
Different in habit

"Go on, Ning-ning."

"No, you were not listening."

"How did you know?"

"I knew."

"Okay, now, Ning-ning, let's try the poem by Wang Wei we read a few weeks ago."

"The one about quietness in the mountain?"

"Yes."

"All right, here it goes:

> Empty hills, no one in sight
> only the sound of someone talking
> last sunlight enters the deep woods
> shining over the green moss again

"You know what it means?" Grandpa asked.

"Grandpa, I wish we were in those deep woods now. Sunshine, green moss, and quiet. No bombing, no hiding like this."

"Yes, that would be nice," he agreed.

"Grandpa?"

"Yes?"

"How do you know the Japanese look like us?"

"I just do."

"No difference at all?"

"No," he hesitated, "except that the Chinese have too much wood and water in them while the Japanese have too much fire and metal."

"What does that mean?"

"Well, people with excessive wood or water in them tend to be too supple, too pliable, too gentle. And people with excessive fire or metal in them? They tend to erupt; they tend to explode and destroy with great violence."

"Really?" Ning-ning marveled. "But Grandpa, we can use water to put out fire and use wood to resist metal, can't we?"

"Yes, but...well, sometimes the fire and metal is just too

84

fierce."

The rumbling outside had subsided. As they were talking, it had become quiet.

He held his breath, waiting, and so did Ning-ning. He knew.

11.

John Rabe, along with Reverend John Magee, another member of the International Committee, was making a tour of the city.

Han was at the wheel of Rabe's car. After leaving the International Committee headquarters on Ninghai Road, the car turned onto Shaanxi Road, then Sun Yat-sen Boulevard, moving cautiously. Rabe caught sight of Magee filming the scenes along the street with his Bolex H-16mm movie camera half hidden in his winter overcoat.

Only a few short minutes later, they saw a phalanx of a hundred or so Japanese troops advancing along the street towards them. Behind this first group of troops was an even larger detachment of at least three to four hundred soldiers shuffling down the street in the distance.

Rabe remained nonplussed as their car was stopped and surrounded instantly. He expected this.

A junior officer barked something in Japanese first, and then in what Rabe would call pidgin Chinese and could only half understand.

Rabe exited the car, and said to the officer in Chinese: "*Waiguoren*," he said, pointing at himself and the others in the car, emphatically, "*Waiguoren, bu shi Zhongguoren*." Foreigners, not Chinese.

The officer barked again, gesturing now that he wanted everybody to get out of the car.

Desperate, Rabe pulled out the swastika armband from his overcoat pocket and flashed it excitedly.

The officer's hardened face relaxed. He gestured to the soldiers standing nearby to back away from the car and called out something toward the large detachment of troops that had already drawn closer.

At the head of the long detachment were a few officers on horseback. One of them, middle-aged, and wearing a pair of gold-rimmed glasses, dismounted, strode up to Rabe, and greeted him in German.

"*Ich bin ein Armee Doktor, geschult in Hamburg. Ich liebe Bach und Bethoven.*" ("Me, army doctor, trained in Hamburg. I love Bach and Beethoven.")

"*Hamburg is meine Heimatstadt,*" replied Rabe. ("Hamburg is my hometown.")

"*Es ist eine schoene Stadt!*" ("It is a beautiful city!")

Rabe explained that they were on their way to meet the highest commandant of the Japanese army to deliver a letter.

"*Noch zwei Tage, vielleicht,*" the army doctor said, amiably ("Two more days, perhaps.").

The army doctor gave Rabe a cursory bow. When the Japanese column went on its way, Rabe got back into the car. He told Han to turn into a side street.

"Hurry! We've got to beat them!"

The car raced through the streets. Rabe encountered several large groups of Chinese soldiers, and each time they stopped and Rabe, through the window, tried to convince them to lay down their guns. It would be suicide, he told them, to keep fighting against a larger, better equipped, and fast-advancing army. Rabe told the Chinese soldiers to go to the Foreign Affairs Ministry and the Supreme Court.

Where he thought they would be safe.

12.

Minnie, Helen, and the cafeteria staff were busy preparing breakfast.

The kitchen was filled with so much steam that Minnie had to wipe the lenses of her glasses with a piece of silky cloth every few minutes. She and Helen poured pickled vegetables from a bag into large wooden bowls lined up on a table.

"Have I told you about my trip back to America in 1925?" Minnie asked.

"No. What was it like?" Helen looked up, her eyes glittering with interest.

"Now, here's the story."

It was a visit she'd never forget. Her starry-eyed nieces and nephews were mesmerized by her Chinese stories every night, and her family was amazed when she treated them with such Chinese delicacies as shark fins, bird nests, whatnot, which she had thoughtfully brought home after a prolonged, tempestuous voyage across the Pacific. When she finally presented a plate of *pi dan*, the specially preserved eggs with blackish yolks, and greenish whites, and an exotic, pungent smell, everybody at the table was taken aback with wide-open eyes.

"What is it, auntie?" Emma, her favorite niece, asked.

"It's the thousand-year-old eggs," Minnie teased. That was the dish's English name after all.

"Ugh!" Emma exclaimed, covering her mouth.

And everybody burst out laughing.

"I'd have laughed, too!" enthused Helen. "It's not one of my favorite dishes, either."

"As expected," Minnie concluded, picking up another bag of pickled vegetables, "I was the only one who relished the thousand-year-old egg dish. Nobody else dared even touch it."

A male cook had finished transporting steamy congee from a huge wok into wooden buckets with a big gourd ladle. They were ready to deliver breakfast to various buildings where refugees were staying. When she saw Helen also grabbing a basket filled with steamed bread and pickled vegetables, Minnie was concerned.

"You're sure you can handle that?"

"Don't you worry about me, Miss Hua."

"Mmmm, I still remember that basketball game. You beat us really bad."

As the male cook stood up with two big buckets of steamy congee dangling from a carrying pole on his shoulder, Minnie's eyes fell on the thin ropes connecting the buckets and the pole.

"Can you imagine the embassy people coming by and giving me that rope?

"What for?" Helen had a surprised look on her face.

"In case I decided to leave after all the city gates were closed!"

"Miss Hua, alias Professor Minnie Vautrin, acting dean of Ginling College, scaling the walls of Nanking under a moonless sky!"

They both burst out laughing.

On their way back after delivering breakfast, Minnie, Helen, and the cook followed the little path up to South Hill. From there they could see the sky over Purple Mountain still shrouded in smoke. For too many weeks they had not seen the mountain's majestic beauty.

They saw a young girl, dressed in boys' clothes, strolling slowly under the trees and gazing intently into the branches. Upon hearing their footsteps, the girl turned around.

"Good morning, Miss Hua," the girl bowed, "Hi, Helen."

Helen took Eva's hand in a warm, sisterly manner.

"Good morning, Eva," Minnie replied. "Are you looking for something?"

"Yes," Eva said, shyly.

"What is it?"

"Birds."

Oh, Minnie thought, I've forgotten about the birds. The azure-winged magpie, the spot-necked dove, the ring-necked pheasant, and oh, the little blue kingfisher, a feathered jewel of a bird which visits the campus occasionally in search of small fish. Even in winter, Ginling has been the favorite destination for many birds, the fan-tailed warblers, streak-eyed wagtails, gray starlings, and bohemian waxwings....

They must have all gone in search of quieter, more hospitable habitats now. Who would blame them?

"Have you found any?" Minnie asked curiously.

"No," Eva shook her head. "I remember seeing lots of birds, all kinds, on campus. Even in winter."

"Yes, I miss them, too."

"Helen," Eva continued, "remember Ning-ning's grandpa has a skylark? Oh, you should listen to him singing. It gives you a kind of feeling. I don't know how to put it. A kind of joy, I suppose."

Eva's eyes sparkled with rapture as she talked. Then she grew thoughtful.

"Miss Hua," Eva turned to her, hesitantly, "do you think it's sinful of me to be looking for something... something to give me joy?"

Minnie was surprised by the question, "What on earth put that thought in your head?"

"Well, you know, with the war going on... " Eva faltered.

"Hmmm," Minnie thought for a moment and said, "remember the Noah's Ark story you read in Bible class?"

"Yes. Miss Ling taught us that."

"Why do you think God instructed Noah to place a pair of every kind of animal, pigs, dogs, chickens, sheep, and birds, you know, in the ark?"

"So that they will not be destroyed in the flood?"

"Yes, and so that God's children would not live in a boring, lonely world, so that there would be joy in the world, right?"

"I see," Eva murmured.

"And do you remember what Noah did to find out whether the flood had finally receded?" interjected Helen.

"He sent out a raven and a dove, and only the dove came back with an olive branch in its beak." Eva sounded more confident this time.

"Exactly!" exclaimed Minnie. The girl has taken Bible class to heart.

"I see what you mean." A smile brightened up Eva's eyes again.

"You'll need lots of luck to find any birds on campus now, though," said Helen, her arms still around Eva's shoulders.

"That's true," said Minnie warmly. "But remember that the

birds will come back, sooner or later. Trust me on this."

Eva bowed again as they turned to leave.

"What a girl," Helen said at last once they were on their way again. "When I found her three years ago, her old, blind grandma wouldn't let her come to our Homecraft School no matter what. The old woman actually believed that Eva had brought the family some real bad luck."

Minnie only shook her head.

As they got closer to the Quad, the center of the college, they saw Big Wang, a groundskeeper, running toward them.

"What's it?" Minnie asked.

"The Japanese! Some Japanese soldiers are on West Hill!"

Minnie suddenly felt goosebumps spreading over her body. She labored to breathe.

"How did they get in?" She asked.

"Nobody knows. They must have scaled the walls."

"Scaled the walls!" She gave Helen an ashen look.

They hurried in the direction of West Hill.

13.

At the University of Nanking Hospital, Dr. Robert Wilson had just finished operating on a patient who had suffered a severe eye injury from an exploding bomb several days earlier.

It was a close call. He had to remove the patient's left eye in order to save the other one. When he was about halfway through the surgery, a shell landed about fifty yards away from the hospital and rocked the ground underneath him with a thunderous explosion. Startled, he looked up and, through the window facing him, saw a dark cloud billowing into the sky. He looked at Iva, the 67-year-old American nurse and the three other young Chinese nurses who were assisting him. They weren't hurt, but they were all visibly shaken.

"Thank God," he muttered.

"Shall we continue, doc?" Iva asked, her voice quivering.

Even though he had started to work as a surgeon at the hospital only two years ago, Dr. Wilson felt perfectly at home in Nanking. After all, he had been born here thirty-one years ago into a family of Methodist missionaries. His uncle, John Ferguson, was the founder of the University of Nanking; his father, an ordained minister, had taught at a middle school in Nanking for many years; and his mother, who had a gift for languages, had run a missionary school of her own.

Robert Wilson had grown up in Nanking nourished by a

happy, loving, intellectually fertile environment. He completed his undergraduate education at Princeton on a scholarship and earned his M.D. from Harvard Medical School. He even taught and worked at a few places in New England. But when he returned to Nanking with his bride, Marjorie, it was like coming home.

For the first two years after their return, they led an idyllic life of elaborate dinners, elegant tea parties and receptions, festive gatherings, and quiet evenings reading some of the great classics of Chinese literature. But over the past three months? Nothing but sirens, air raids, explosions, fires, injury, and death. Marjorie had taken Elizabeth, their infant daughter, back to America, and he was glad that they were safe. Nanking was a hideous place now, to be sure, but it was still his home. He had already operated on so many soldiers and civilians wounded in battles and in aerial bombings he had lost track of time. Each day blended in with the next.

After finishing with the solider with the eye injury, Wilson's next patient was an officer who had been hit by shrapnel while en route to the hospital on a stretcher. The bomb, which landed only just outside the hospital, wounded another young soldier and killed two others.

The wounded officer was lying on the operating table. His eyes were closed, his chest heaving unevenly. Wilson examined his head and face, which was covered with smoke, dust, and dried blood. There was a small piece of metal shrapnel lodged in his head, surrounded by bloodstained and matted hair.

He proceeded to cut away the officer's torn, bloodstained uniform.

Something on the officer's abdomen, about two or three

inches to the left of his navel, caught the doctor's eye: a birthmark, purple, no bigger than small silver coin, but in the shape of a bird with outstretched wings. Wilson had never seen such an unusual birthmark before.

"Isn't that something?" he said to Iva.

In addition to the metal shrapnel lodged in his head, the officer had sustained two other wounds: a bullet hole through his left hand and a gaping flesh wound, about the size of an egg, on his right thigh, which exposed flesh and muscle. It was not life-threatening.

The patients came and went. The hours passed. The shadows grew long. Sunlight began to fade. Looking up from the last operation, Dr. Wilson glimpsed the moon, nearly full, rising over Purple Mountain. The moon was so quiet, serene, and so indescribably beautiful. Yet its majestic light illuminated a darkened, nearly deserted Nanking. Now a city of shadows that had never seen such sorry, despair, and a mortal fear of what would happen tomorrow. Wilson's heart ached.

As he turned to make a final round of the patients before leaving the hospital for home, the first two lines of Li Po's "Longing," a favorite poem of his, came to mind:

> Sunlight begins to fade
>   mist fills the flowers
> The moon as white as silk
>   weeps and cannot sleep

Tuesday

December 14, 1937
The Second Day

14.

Ning-ning woke up in darkness.

Slowly, she sat up carefully, propping open the lid of the coffin with the umbrella, climbed out, and reached underneath Grandpa's bed to get breakfast.

The cold, steamed buns smelled alright, thanks in part to the cold December weather, but it had lost most of its original moisture and now had a rather dry, powdery texture to it. It would take a mouthful of water—cold, unboiled water—to wash down each small bite.

Grandpa's teeth had all but gone. He had to break off a tiny piece of the bun with his shivering fingers, put it into his mouth, and chew slowly and cautiously.

"Are you okay, Grandpa," Ning-ning asked, busy chewing by his bedside.

"Mmmm."

This was the second day since the Japanese had marched in. The air raids had stopped. So did the deafening explosions erupting all around Purple Mountain, in the city, or in the outlying neighborhoods.

When the first air raids began three months ago, to the most recent bombing and shelling of the past couple of days, it was, Ning-ning thought, not unlike the excitement before, during, and after Chinese New Year.

Even in the days before the New Year's, Ning-ning would hear firecrackers crackling and sputtering along nearby streets and alleys, mostly from young children who couldn't wait for the festival to begin.

The sound of firecrackers would pick up momentum until the New Year, when the city was transformed into a sea of blazing firecrackers, happy-jolly feasts, and blissful greetings.

The excitement would wane gradually after the New Year's Day until people had settled down to the same old routine of everyday life.

Young as she was, Ning-ning felt this comparison of hers rather absurd. She knew that firecrackers were supposed to scare away evil spirits and ring in good fortune for the coming year. The bombing and shelling from the Japanese, however, had brought nothing but destruction, death, and despair. She hated it. Deep down she knew she hated it.

Her eyes moistened again as the memories came flooding back.

Mama was the talented, resourceful chef. Papa was cutting meat, scaling fish, and washing vegetables nonstop. Grandpa was busy writing holiday blessings on those huge red scrolls for all the neighbors, and Ning-ning herself, Grandpa's proud, capable assistant, was in charge of the paper and ink.

The family went together to the Temple of Confucius to see the dragon dances, parades, opera performances, festive lanterns glowing, hanging from every building and tree, and lamp-lit boats drifting dreamily along the Qinhuai River. From her vantage point atop Papa's shoulders, Ning-ning could see it all clearly. She would give anything to relive those happy moments again.

Now, they had heard troops marching through their neighborhood, smashing windows and breaking down doors, amid the sound of people screaming. From all directions along Sun Yat-sen Boulevard, sporadic gunshots echoed in the crisp December air. So far, though, no Japanese soldiers had wandered into the sidestreet, down their alley, into their yard, up the stairs, and poked their face through their door. So far.

"Grandpa." Ning-ning said, coming out of her reverie.

"Yes?" Grandpa said, as he took a sip of water from a small cup.

"Why haven't we heard from Papa and Mama for so long?"

Grandpa paused, "Well, I told you...what I mean is that they probably sent us several letters already, from Hankou or Chunking, someplace safe. But with the war going on and the mess here—"

"So you mean their letters are on the way here?" Grandpa could hear the excited tone in her voice.

"Any day now, I guess," Grandpa replied.

"Are you sure?"

"I'm sure," Grandpa added with emphasis.

15.

The first thing Dr. Wilson did upon arriving at the hospital in the morning was to make a round to check on all the patients.

Most of the patients in the ward were still asleep, though many were already awake and in the middle of their breakfasts: rice congee. The patients greeted him with a cursory nod of the head or a with a warm smile.

Nearing the bed of the man with the bird-shaped birthmark, he noticed that the officer, his head still wrapped in layers of white bandages, had opened his eyes and was quite alert, and in the middle of a conversation with the young, boyish patient lying in the next bed.

"You're doing okay?" Dr. Wilson asked both men.

"Yeah," replied the older patient in a gravely voice. He struggled to move his good arm out from under the quilt in order to shake Wilson's hand, but instead winced in pain. He froze for a moment and then put his arm back.

"You'll be fine," Dr. Wilson reassured. "In a few days, both of you will be out of here."

"Really?" the younger patient asked, a sparkle in his eyes.

"Absolutely."

"That's wonderful!" exclaimed the younger patient again. "Isn't that wonderful, Colonel... Mr. Ling?"

"Mmmm."

16.

Although he was wearing a thick winter coat and had his leather belt buckled tight around his waist to keep the warmth inside, Second Lieutenant Kuroda still felt tired and cold.

The sun was shining, but it was a very cold day, the end of his fourth month in China. It had been hell. The worst, of course, was being humiliated by Lieutenant Colonel Tajima in front of his whole platoon yesterday morning. True, there was an impromptu victory celebration he, together with some of his fellow soldiers had held last night. Although it had managed to cheer him up, the way in which it ended just dampened his spirits even more. He exhaled deeply into the cold morning air.

His platoon had found a storage area in an office building which contained a large amount of canned goods and other food. What really thrilled them, though, were the few cases of aged spirits and red-colored liquor. What good fortune they were having! After having their spoils transported back to a small residential building where his platoon was camping, Kuroda decided to have a celebration. They set up a memorial tablet with the names of their fallen comrades hastily inscribed on it, and surrounded it with a few lighted candles, incense sticks, and offerings of water and the canned food they had just brought home. They took turns bowing at the makeshift altar, heated up the aged spirits in pots, drank, and sang old folksongs:

A full cup taken
Of wine.
Into the black jug
Pour it
Into the white jug
Pour it
With one's lover
When
Giving
Taking
The Heart
How does it feel?

Kuroda knew the sexual double entendre in this song of two lovers exchanging cups of wine. It put him in the mood and he began to howl with everybody else with wild abandon:

To a flowering cherry
The stallion why have you tied?
The horse, becoming restless
Will shake off the flowers

How he would love to be that stallion now and shake off some flowers from the tree. Instead, he was stuck here in a war in a foreign country. How he missed the flowering cherry trees in his home village in Kuma County in south central Kyushu. Would he ever be able to go back home? To his aged parents? And to Miyoko, his new bride?

At the thought of Miyoko, Kuroda felt a rush of joy leaping from his heart into his body. Oh, Miyoko, how I miss you!

The night before he was to leave for China, only days after their wedding, Miyoko didn't say a word. They had made love for a long time. He had never thought that a woman could be possessed with such passion. Now, Miyoko was so different from the shy girl on their wedding night—who had seemed so shocked and so confused by it all. Now, she was so attentive to his needs-his wants, in every possible way. From the way her body arched as she welcomed his embrace, to the way her hands caressed his back, to the way they moved together as one while she moaned from someplace deep inside her, Kuroda knew that she was as eager to receive as she was to give.

Afterwards, her eyes glistened with tears as she lay by his side. He had noticed but did not say a word or even ask why she was crying. What could he have said? What could she have said? He was to leave for China in the morning. It was not a woman's place to talk about such things anyway.

Now tears welled in Kuroda's eyes. Will I ever see her again? What will happen if I end up dead in China? What would she do then? Miyoko-and otousan, and okaa-san, waiting for my return each day even though I lie rotting on the ground.

The soldiers were still singing with gusto:

> You and I are cherry blossoms
> of the same year
> Even if we're far apart
> when our petals fall
> We'll bloom again in the treetops
> of the Capital's Yasukuni Shrine.

What an honor it would be if he could bloom again as a cherry blossom at the Yasukuni Shrine in Tokyo. That way he would live again. That way he would have truly honored his aged parents, his hometown, and Miyoko, of course.

Yet he had hesitated, faltered, if only for a few fleeting moments early yesterday morning. He remembered clearly the many rows of Chinese prisoners with heads bowed.

His hesitation had been noticed-exploited-by Lieutenant Colonel Tajima in front of everyone. What could he do to undo the shame he had brought upon himself? The prisoners had sang, in defiance of what? Kuroda gave the order after Tajima and Nakamoto had departed. Not a single prisoner was spared. Was the massive bloodletting enough to thoroughly purge his shame?

Ueno, one of his buddies from the same county, started to sing "The Difficult Bride,"

> The one gotten last night
> The bride
> The next day
> When possessing her
> Does the cunt stink?
> Or hasn't it any hair
> Can she not
> Raise herself high enough?

This verse threw everyone in the room into a frenzy. They all jumped up, formed a circle, as if each were holding a rope attached to a heavy log-pounder held vertically, pulled and let slack alternately, and moved in a steady rhythm, howling the refrain in chorus after Ueno's lead:

> If she cannot
> Rise high enough
> A quilt underneath
> Try to place
> Even if with that
> It is not enough
> During the month of August
> Some chestnut-burs
> Pick up
> And these under her buttocks
> Try to place
> If even that
> Is not enough
> With a frame
> Hoist her up

"We've taken Nanking!" Kuroda shouted at last. "The war is over. And we will all be home soon!"

The men carried on well into the night.

Banzai! They all cheered. Too loudly.

The door to the room burst open. Captain Akiyama poked is head in and yelled in disgust:

"Why don't you all shut up and go to bed or I'll have you skinned! The fight will continue tomorrow, and the day after tomorrow! Who do you think you are?"

They all froze in mid-song. It was as if a basin of icy water had been poured on them. Looking at the floor, they scurried to their respective corners and huddled in silence.

It was no surprise then that Kuroda still felt a bit sleepy this morning when his company stopped at a compound along a main street a few kilometers into the Safety Zone. The compound was comprised of three large two-story buildings, which were connected by a hallway, and a cooking area in the center quadrangle. An elementary or middle school perhaps?

Captain Akiyama barked some orders and soldiers orderly flooded into the compound. No one could get in or out. Eight large-caliber machine guns were set up on tripods and pointed toward the buildings. The captain split up the company so that each platoon was responsible for searching one building.

Kuroda's platoon kicked open the door to the building on the right. Right away they found dozens of Chinese civilians huddled pathetically in several rooms on the first floor. Kuroda saw their faces, twisted by shock and fear.

A large room was found downstairs holding as many as a hundred people.

"Take them down there. All of them." Captain Akiyama barked.

Some of the Chinese being herded downstairs looked much older than otousan and okaa-san. They teetered along, leaning feebly on their walking sticks. Small children shuffled quietly along. Even babies in the arms of their mothers didn't make any noise.

Kuroda gave orders to separate all the young men who looked like they could be soldiers. They would be taken to a separate room for interrogation. As the young men were singled out by Kuroda's men, they howled in protest:

"*Bu shi!*" ("I'm not!")

"*Bu dui!*" ("It's a mistake!")

But their protests were in vain as the bayonets pressed in closer.

"*Ni!*" ("You!") Ueno would call out in Chinese, dragging a young man out from the crowd.

"*Ni guo lai!*" ("Come over!") Ueno barked again.

The young Chinese men were taken to an interrogation room about ten at a time. They were surrounded by soldiers and searched. Any valuables or other possessions were confiscated.

"You're a soldier, aren't you?" Ueno asked, mechanically.

A young Chinese man, terrified and confused, struggled to come up with an answer to try and save himself. Ueno nodded to the soldiers in the room, who promptly beat and kicked the young man. He fell to the floor, but he was held down, his arm twisted behind his back. His genitals were poked mercilessly with a stick. Held down, he squealed like a pig that had just been skewered on a spit.

Some of the young men being questioned were indeed former soldiers. They were still wearing underclothing with tags bearing the name of their battalion or company. Meekly, they were herded into another holding room.

Around noon the interrogations were over. Kuroda's platoon had detained close to three hundred men they suspected were soldiers. He was quite pleased when he saw that the other two platoons had rounded up only about five hundred between them.

Eight or nine hundred prisoners altogether! Not an insignificant number at all. The prisoners were assembled outside in the quad where they filled it up completely.

As Kuroda sat down to lunch nearby, he realized, of course, that it was not as big a number as those prisoners he encountered in the early morning hours two days ago when they blasted through the south city gate. There were several thousand then, just sitting there, waiting to be taken.

The memory brought back the same burning sense of shame again. Kuroda had hesitated awkwardly and bungled getting all the prisoners to line up in an orderly way, leaving the door open for Tajima to exploit his inexperience by taking nine heads right in front of him. Surely Kuroda had redeemed himself by ordering the bloodbath which followed.

What a sight it had been. Kuroda had ordered his soldiers to stand at the front of each line of prisoners, and, with bayonets at the ready, they made sport of who could cut their way through an entire line of men first. Having been stabbed or slashed, the men fell but did not die. More troops came down the line and finished them off, as well as any of those who tried to break out of their formation and flee. It was ritualistic slaughter. There were no bullets. The men were cut to pieces, impaled, eyes skewered, abdomens sliced open, and jugular veins severed by one decisive bayonet thrust. Blood sprayed in all directions, then poured forth in a relentless crimson torrent as the bodies writhed and thrashed in the dirt before they at last lay still. It was he, Kuroda, who had given the order.

Kuroda had his misgivings about the Chinese: Why don't they fight? Surely dying in battle was more honorable than being cut down like this.

After lunch, Captain Akiyama relayed an order from Lieutenant Colonel Tajima: All of the suspected soldiers in the quad were to be taken to Lotus Lake and shot, their bodies dumped into the water.

The prisoners were made to line up in five columns. Those

in the two outermost columns were tied to each other with downed electrical and telephone wire gathered from the street. Under Kuroda's watchful eye, this procession of prisoners, eight to nine hundred strong, marched northeastward toward Lotus Gate, which was in the opposite direction of the Safety Zone. The big machines guns were cleared from the quad.

It had become overcast now, and the wind was blowing fiercely. These Chinese, thought Kuroda again, did they have any idea what was going to happen to them? What if they all bolted at the same time? No, Kuroda concluded, they didn't have the will left to fight.

As it happened, Lotus Gate was blocked by huge piles of sandbags left behind by retreating Chinese troops. Lotus Lake was outside the gate. Now Captain Akiyama surveyed the situation: there was no way to clear away the sandbags and open the gate in time to carry out the order. Akiyama decided to dispose of the prisoners on the spot.

At the foot of the tall wall on the right side of Lotus Gate was an immense pit. It must have resulted from the digging up of dirt to fill the sandbags. While not deep, it was both long and broad. The prisoners were told to file along the narrow strip of dirt which lay between the wall behind them and the pit in front of them. Then they were told to go down into the pit. The eight big machine guns, which had been taken from the quad, were now set up opposite the wall, pointing downward into the pit.

It was then that the young Chinese men suddenly awakened from their stupor. Right away a dozen or so tried to break free and run, but they were caught and stabbed immediately, then thrown into the pit. Some of the other Chinese soldiers turned to their captors and tossed them their pens, cigarettes, and whatever small, secret items had remained hidden somewhere in their clothes, mumbling incoherently.

"Ha, ha! We're getting an allowance from the Chinese!" Ueno joked. "*Tai chi le!*" ("Too late!")

A man in the tied-together line close to Kuroda tossed him his watch. How could it have escaped the early search? The watch fell to the ground at Kuroda's feet. The man looked up forlornly for a moment, then, with eyes devoid of emotion, plodded on, pushed down into the pit by Ueno.

Another man in his thirties produced a red string from his pocket where he seemed to cut and reattach it several times over. Then, he played with a small ball, making it disappear in his mouth and reappear behind his neck over and over again. Even though his hands shook uncontrollably, the man's skills were sufficient to maintain the illusion. Kuroda and his comrades were quite amused and they roared with laughter.

As he was stepping into the pit, the magician had one more trick. He pulled out a match then struck it against his fingernail to light. The feeble flame flickered, but as the man was preparing to bring the flame to his mouth, it was blown out by a sudden gust of wind. The man stood there, holding the smoldering match in his fingers as a feeble puff of grey smoke hung pathetically in the air in front of his face.

Kuroda and his men were beside themselves with laughter and roared uncontrollably. They were sure this man would eat fire, or walk into an erupting volcano, if it could save his life.

"Can you make yourself disappear?" Ueno taunted.

The man, his face expressionless, descended into the pit. His arms were at his sides, but he did not release the match from between his fingers.

All the captives were in the enormous pit now. Their eyes glanced up at the machine guns and the men standing behind them, poised at the edge of the pit. What were they thinking? Kuroda wondered. Those who get first will be the lucky ones.

"Fire!" Captain Akiyama said, calmly and without hesitation.

Instantly, all eight machine-guns roared to life in a deafening cacophony.

The men who were hit first were indeed the lucky ones. Their limp bodies were hurled aside in panic or trampled upon as the men in the pit clambered instinctively to escape certain death. Uniforms were ripped to pieces by flying bullets as blood erupted from gaping, smoking holes. Bits of burnt, torn flesh, shattered skulls, and exploding brains flew into the air. The machine guns thundered on. The empty, smoking shell casings rolled about the feet of Akiyama's men as they fired: left and right, up and down.

Kuroda hastily moved back, but his uniform was sticky as splashes of blood and flesh rained down.

A minute later, Akiyama's voice could be heard: "Cease fire!"

Acrid smoke rose up from the machine guns, and for a moment there was silence. Then they heard the ghastly moans and primal shrieks which rose from the pit, echoed along the wall, and hung in the air overhead.

The machine gun operators breathed hard, but did not take their eyes away from the cross-hairs in front of them.

"Fire!" Akiyama ordered again, and the guns erupted to life once more.

It was not until the captain had paused again after giving the order for a third time, that, finally, there was no sound coming from the pit.

They'd all gone to the other world now, Kuroda thought as he joined in to cover up the bodies with dirt. They used the shovels the Chinese soldiers had used to fill the sandbags with dirt. Kuroda had thought to point out to Akiyama that the layer of dirt covering the bodies was too thin. Once the bodies had stiffened up in the sun they would poke through the dirt like some macabre garden. Kuroda decided to keep the thought to himself.

An hour later, Kuroda's company joined the other units of the battalion and marched northward in the direction of Lower Pass Dock. Soon they came upon the smoking remnants of a burned out three-story building. As they drew closer, Kuroda could see that the ground was littered with the twisted, broken, and burned bodies of dozens of men. Another battalion had taken about a hundred suspected Chinese soldiers up to the roof before setting the building on fire right under their feet with gasoline poured into every room. Those who did not die from the acrid smoke leapt to their deaths engulfed in flames.

Kuroda suddenly felt someone staring at him. He turned his head slowly to the right and noticed Lieutenant Colonel Tajima, astride a tall horse by the roadside, inspecting the procession of troops as they continued to march.

Next to Tajima, atop another grand, ebony horse, was another officer. He looked familiar, with a cold, piercing gaze behind a pair of gold-rimmed glasses, and a small, square moustache between the nose and tightened lips. It was Brigadier General Nakamoto. The general had been there two days ago when Kuroda humiliated himself with his momentary hesitation.

Kuroda quickened his pace to catch up with his comrades, resolving not to bring any more shame upon himself.

17.

John Rabe was touring the city again.

As before, Reverend John Magee, now chairman of the newly founded Nanking Branch of the International Red Cross Committee, was with him, together with Reverend Ernest Forester, an Episcopal minister, and the branch's secretary. Han was again at the wheel.

When members of the Safety Zone committee met early yesterday morning at its headquarters on Ninghai Road, they had come to a quick consensus on the urgent need to establish a branch of the International Red Cross in order to deal with a potential humanitarian disaster not only within the Safety Zone, but also beyond its boundaries. Rabe, of course, knew all of the other members personally. Several of them, such as Magee, Drs. Lewis Smythe, M. S. Bates, Reverend W. P. Mills, and himself, were already on the Safety Zone committee. A few of them, though, were new additions: Ernest Forester, Dr. Robert Wilson of the University of Nanking Hospital, Professor Minnie Vautrin of Ginling College for Women, and two Chinese: Mr. Li Chui-nan of the Chinese Red Cross Society of Nanking, and Pastor Shen Yu-shu.

As they drove, the pale early afternoon sunshine fell listlessly on abandoned equipment, uniforms, and personal belongings which littered the road. Now and again Han would spot a hand grenade lying in the middle of the road, and deftly guide the car around it. A small Red Cross flag, affixed hastily to the car's aerial, fluttered nervously as they drove. Once again Magee used his 16mm motion-picture camera half shielded by his winter overcoat.

Japanese troops were scuffling around the city in groups of ten to twenty, smashing open windows and doors with guns, rocks, and bricks, and looting whatever valuables they could find. Not a single shop or home along Sun Yat-sen Boulevard and Heavenly Peace Road had been spared. Some of the Japanese soldiers dragged their booty away in crates, others forced Chinese laborers to transport for them the stolen goods in rickshaws, carts, or on carrying poles.

Earlier that day, Magee had taken an ambulance full of wounded Chinese soldiers to the Ministry of Foreign Affairs, which had been transformed into a makeshift hospital. After first carrying the most seriously wounded into the hospital on stretchers, they turned to help those who could still manage to walk on their own. They were just half way up the steps when a gang of Japanese soldiers arrived. One of them grabbed the man Magee was helping, jerking hard on his terribly wounded arm and tying his hands behind his back, causing the poor fellow to scream with pain as he was led away to certain death.

"Wild beasts!" Magee was still livid with foaming anger when he recounted the incident later at the Safety Zone committee headquarters.

Rabe told Han to stop so that they could get out of the car and examine the dead bodies sprawled on the sidewalks. Many appeared to be former soldiers dressed in civilian clothes. All had bullet wounds in their backs.

They got back in the car and a few minutes later they arrived at Kiessling & Bader, whose hand-made cheeses and fresh baked breads Rabe had enjoyed for the last ten years. Rabe quickly spotted Herr Kiessling himself arguing furiously with several Japanese soldiers. Rabe leaped from the car even before it had stopped in front of the store.

"What's going on here?" Rabe demanded. He was careful now, projecting his displeasure to the Japanese soldiers while not jeopardizing the safety of his friends with an uncontrollable outburst.

The soldiers in dirty yellow uniforms turned to face him. In their hands were items they had apparently taken from the bakery (and, upstairs, Herr Kiessling's residence): an expensive-looking fur coat, a large, gold-trimmed clock, and a small, exquisitely framed oil painting. The large swastika Kiessling had carefully hung in front of the building had been torn down.

One of the soldiers dropped the bag in his hand, raised his rifle, and moved a step closer to Rabe. Rabe immediately pulled out the swastika armband from his pocket and shook it excitedly in the soldier's face, as he had done before.

"*Herr Hitler*! *Herr Hitler*! Understand?" he roared like a lion, Magee, Forester, and Han stood frozen behind him.

The soldier seemed shocked by the outburst. He stood there, mumbling something in Japanese. Seeing that Rabe didn't understand him, the soldier began to make frantic gestures with his hand, pointing at his mouth and his belly. The soldiers turned to leave, dragging their spoils behind them. When Kiessling made a move to go after them again, Rabe held him back.

"Let them have it," he said. "At least nobody's hurt here."

Up until today, the Japanese soldiers seemed to have shown

more respect for the Germans and their swastika. Rumors were rife that Americans and other Europeans had fared less fortunately. Several American cars and trucks had been taken and commandeered, their flags ripped off and thrown to the ground. But they were still alive. The Japanese were not killing them. Things could take a turn for the worse, even for a German.

Not long after they had left Kiessling the bakery, Rabe and his colleagues saw a large group of Chinese, as many has two hundred perhaps, all being loaded onto trucks with hands tied behind their backs. How could the Japanese do that within the Safety Zone! Rabe was infuriated.

But Magee was the first to exit the car this time. "Where are you taking them?" he demanded. Rabe and Forester followed.

The soldiers kept busy pushing the Chinese onto the trucks.

"Why?" Magee asked again.

Except for some mumbling and a few menacing stares, they received no reply.

"You can't simply take them like this!" protested Forester. "These are civilians. Do they look like soldiers?"

But all protests fell on deaf ears. The truck engines roared to life, the transmissions clattered, and the tires rumbled away in the dirt, leaving Rabe and his colleagues behind in a swirling cloud of dust.

After a long pause, they moved silently toward the car. Their next stop was the Ministry of Justice, where yesterday they had left about one thousand disarmed soldiers. As they entered the compound, they saw only a few dozen Chinese soldiers, many seriously wounded, lying helpless on the ground or huddling together in front of the building. Rabe exited the car and walked up to one man, leaning against the wall.

"Where are the others?" Rabe asked.

"They've just been tied up and taken away," mumbled the wounded soldier.

"When?"

"About ten minutes ago."

"To where?"

The man gestured forlornly to the gate. Clearly he did not know.

"How—"

Rabe was cut short. The compound echoed with machine-gun fire roaring and reverberating from all sides. Rabe crouched, instinctively, as did the other men, but they realized that the shots were close by, just outside the Ministry of Justice compound.

Rabe stood there, utterly shaken. He immediately realized the gravity of what he had done: It was he who had told the retreating Chinese soldiers to lay down their arms. Yet the Japanese soldiers had murdered them in cold blood.

Rabe and his men stared at each other. When at last the guns stopped, their ears rang amid the silence.

They all got back into the car, their faces contorted with horror. As the car started to move again, Rabe noticed the small leaflet lying on the floor of the car near his feet. He picked it up:

> All surrendered soldiers and the civilian
> population will be treated humanely in all respects ....

He tore the leaflet to pieces, threw the shreds into the air, and watched them flutter into the air as the car drove away.

When the men finally returned to the Safety Zone headquarters at 5 Ninghai Road, they were exhausted and disheartened. The western sky was still hanging on to the last rays of the setting sun before giving itself over to the coming darkness.

They were told that several refugee centers in the city were facing dangerous food shortages.

Magee, Forester, and a few other committee members decided to deliver sacks of rice to those centers right away.

Rabe arranged to have seven seriously wounded people, who had been lying in the headquarters courtyard for hours, transported to the University of Nanking Hospital.

Rabe's heart ached at the sight of a kid who had been shot in the lower leg. The burned, acrid would and the boy's blood-stained pants told him that the wound was serious. The boy's leg would surely be lost. When Rabe picked him up and placed him in the back seat of his own car, the half-conscious boy cringed but did not make sound.

The sun had all but disappeared. Night enveloped the car as Rabe raced toward the Drum Tower, where the University Hospital was located.

"You'll be fine," he reassured the boy.

18.

Ning-ning was about to clear up "supper things" from Grandpa's bedside when they heard a truck screeching to a halt and a sudden, loud commotion not too far away:

People—Japanese troops?—scuffling around, kicking doors, smashing windows, yelling or cussing in a tongue either too rough or too strange to be intelligible to her. She could hear the sounds of pitiable begging and groaning, trailing off into a long, desperate wail. A shot rang out.

Her hands, holding the cups and a bottle of pickled vegetables, trembled.

"Hurry!" Grandpa whispered, "back to your hideout!"

Whatever it was, it was getting closer. Heavy, booted feet could be heard shuffling in the alley outside. More rough yelling in a strange tongue.

Ning-ning climbed up and fell over into the coffin. Before she had let the lid fall, she heard Grandpa whispering again:

"Don't move, and don't make any noise, no matter what!"

She lay there in darkness, motionless, feeling her heart beating wildly, a sickening knot developing in the pit of her stomach.

The commotion outside was getting closer, and more furious. It moved from right outside to right underneath her! The sound of kicking, smashing, yelling, muffled cries from—a woman's voice?

"Cover your ears! Ning-ning!" she heard Grandpa's voice coming through.

She put an index finger into each ear and pushed so hard that she could feel her arms trembling. She closed her eyes tight. The commotion below raged on. She could feel it. The whole building shook. The reverberations reached her in her dark hiding place and bounced back and forth, sending her mind spinning. There was a loud gunshot: BANG! Ning-ning jumped at the sound, shaking uncontrollably.

She could feel something else: a heavy, hurried pounding on the flight of wooden steps leading upstairs, to her home. Instantly there was a loud crack of wood as the door was kicked flying open on its hinges, striking the wall, and bouncing back. Ning-ning froze, holding her breath. There were shuffling sounds as feet went from one room to another. Things in the house were being thrown about.

There was silence. Silence.

More shuffling. But then she heard it: footsteps going back down the stairs.

Silently, Ning-ning opened her mouth and gasped for air. She heard more furious commotion going on downstairs, then a loud report: BANG! Like a firecracker had just gone off indoors.

More silence.

Ning-ning removed her fingers from her ears slowly.

She wanted to push open the lid and jump out of the cramped, smothering coffin.

"Ning-ning." It was Grandpa's voice. Like a whisper.

"Grandpa?"

"Are you all right?"

"Yes. And you?"

"Mmmm."

"Can I get—?"

"Not yet."

"What have they done to our home?"

"Broken a few things, that's all."

"You saw them?"

"No."

"Didn't they come in?"

"Yes."

"Did they do anything to hurt you?"

"No. Probably too scared by the sight of an ugly old man in bed, mouth wide-open, must have been dead for—"

"Grandpa!"

"—a while. And the black coffin over there? They got out of here quick.

"Oh, stop it, Grandpa!" But she allowed herself to giggle slightly.

"The Japanese, you know," Grandpa continued, "are like us Chinese. They are not too fond of dead old men and black coffins."

"You're still alive, Grandpa!"

"I know."

"Grandpa?" she asked, after a pause. "What happened downstairs?"

Grandpa didn't answer.

"What happened?"

"I don't know."

"I heard something like a gun shot."

"Oh?"

"Didn't you hear it? It must be very bad."

"Yes, very bad," Grandpa murmured.

"How bad? Are Auntie Huang, uncle, and the twins... okay?"

"I don't know."

Ning-ning could hear Grandpa sniffling.

"I think they've gone." He said.

"Who?"

"The Japanese."

"Oh."

Slowly, carefully, Ning-ning pushed open the lid, and climbed out of the coffin.

She threw herself onto Grandpa's bedside, gave him her hands, and he took her hands in his. They held each other for a long time. Grandpa took one of his hands and brushed her short hair lovingly.

It was early evening, and the room was dim. Ning-ning could make out the mess sprawled in the main room. As she tiptoed into the room, she could picture the same mess inside her own small room and Mama and Papa's bedroom without even setting foot there. She turned her gaze toward the open front door.

"Ning-ning?" Grandpa whispered. "Don't!"

"I won't." She would be too scared to go down there by herself. But poor Auntie Huang, uncle, the twins.

Suddenly, she heard a tap, tap, tap, on the windowpane, soft and almost inaudible. She heard it again. Tap. Tap. Tap.

She tiptoed toward the window. They were on the second floor. Auntie Huang?

Tap. Tap. Tap. Tap.

She unlocked the window and swung it open slowly.

Ning-ning's face lit up with joy.

"Hey Kiddo!" she exclaimed. There, perched on the outside windowsill, was Larkie. She gave the bird her open palms. Larkie leapt onto them blithely.

"What is it?" asked Grandpa.

"Larkie!"

"What?" She could hear the excitement in Grandpa's voice.

After closing the window with her elbow, Ning-ning tip-toed back to Grandpa's bedside.

"Larkie's back!" she announced, and brought the bird in front of Grandpa.

Grandpa held out his palms, Larkie leapt onto them, tilted his little head to one side first, then to the other, fixing his child-like gaze on Grandpa.

"Oh, my little precious." Grandpa's hands were shaking, "My little precious is home again."

Ning-ning went to fetch his cage. Inside was the small wooden saucer with rice still in it.

"Easy, easy," she said as they watched Larkie relishing his meal inside the cage. "Don't overstuff yourself."

"My little precious must have been starved," Grandpa murmured, tenderly, "and scared too."

"Kiddo," she said, "you'll never go hungry again from now on. I'll take care of you. Promise."

Larkie looked up, his beady, shiny eyes searched her face, and, as if convinced, he resumed pecking inside the small wooden saucer, making a content, joyous twittering noise now and again.

19.

Nakamoto, on horseback, had just returned to his headquarters, a large, gated residence inside the walls of Nanking. Night was falling.

It was a two-story building of Western architectural style with a steep, dark-tiled roof, beige stucco walls, and a porch supported by imposing columns. The gate itself was wide enough for a car to drive through, and the road gently wound its way through a small front garden to the porch. A large-bowled fountain stood in the middle of the garden, and poised on the rim of the bowl was a statue of a short, curly-haired boy. No water trickled from between his legs, however, and the water in the bowl was green with algae. The surrounding grass was brown and dry, with only the faintest hint of green still left in pockets of lawn next to the house.

Nakamoto's suite was on the second floor. It was a spacious bedroom with its own private bath and an adjacent study with a large mahogany desk and an antique reading lamp, and a few tall bookshelves. Downstairs was a cozy sitting room with an elegant Western sofa, cushioned, high-backed chairs, tables, and antique lamps and clocks. A marbled fireplace served as the focal point of the room, and several tastefully framed oil paintings, mostly western landscapes, covered the walls. An adjoining dining room held a large table which could seat eight people comfortably.

Zenba, together with several other staff members took the other three rooms on the second floor, while the remaining rooms downstairs were occupied by some junior officers.

"Get my bath ready, now!" Nakamoto barked as he dismounted. His feet had not even touched the ground.

"Yes, sir!" Zenba replied, jumping off his horse, too. "It'll be ready in a minute!"

As he strode toward the front steps, Nakamoto caught sight of something crawling slowly near the foot of the wall next to the house. He stopped.

It was a toad.

A huge, ugly green toad! The very sight of its earthy, crinkled, leprous skin made him shiver with repulsion.

The toad stopped; its tiny, unblinking eyes were fixed straight ahead, unmoving.

Nakamoto's hand moved to his sword.

"Get rid of that ugly thing!" he gestured to Zenba.

Upstairs, Nakamoto stepped into the huge, white porcelain bathtub filled with clean, steaming hot water. As he eased back in the tub lazily, he relished the feeling of being carried afloat in the water. As the heat of the water penetrated his skin, a delicious sensation permeated every fiber of his body. He was being transported far away, to another world filled with tantalizing thoughts and a soft, tinkling sound arising from somewhere deep inside his memory. He closed his eyes, relishing the memory again.

A moment later he was brought back to reality by a boisterous uproar. Voices could be heard down the hall singing:

> The one gotten last night
> The bride
> The next day
> When possessing her
> Does the cunt stink?

Nakamoto reached for a bar of soap and began to wash and scrub himself.

> If all of that
> Is not enough
> This time if it smells
> To the limit
> If to that extent
> The cunt stinks
> If it stinks that much
> The cunt
> I will tell you a way
> To avoid it.
> Cook some salted codfish
> Leach it
> And put it
> In a washing tub.

Nakamoto stared at the water. On its surface floated a thick layer of tiny, soapy bubbles that glittered faintly in the dim lamplight. The joyous singing went on:

Even if this
Is not enough
Grind some spice and pepper
Into powder
And this is into the private part
Try putting
Nearly all the odor
Will disappear.

Nakamoto shook his head. Spice and pepper powder? That must burn as painfully as....

Damn! Nakamoto fell back in the tub listlessly and buried his body deep in the hot water again. He shivered suddenly, and could feel the water lapping against his chest and chin as a flood of hateful memories flooded back to haunt him yet again.

It is the hand of a giggling woman, reaching out from the doorway of a shabby inn tucked away in a dark, back alley.

The soft hand leads a sheepish, first-year cadet into a dimly-lit room. Having been brutalized for months by sadistic officers and upperclassmen, the young cadet is seeking comfort and tenderness at last.

But he awakes the following morning, only to see, in the glaring light of the morning sun streaming in through the open shoji screen, a hideous, toad-like face, with disheveled hair, and a limp mouth filled with crooked, yellow teeth. It is grinning, leering at him, and giggling.

The cadet shuts himself in the bathroom, pouring salt into a bowl of water, dipping a small towel into the bowl, and with the salty wet towel, feverishly wiping the stinky crust from his manhood.

The cadet leaves the shabby inn in the dark, back alley on a moonless night with a bloody sword in hand.

Spice and pepper powder in the private part! The brigadier general grinned, shook his head. That must hurt even worse than salt!

The bath was finally over. Nakamoto put on his kimono. He felt so clean, like he had been many years ago, before he had become a cadet at Ichigaya Military Academy. Now, he was still like the cute little son of *okaa-san*!

The last time he saw okaa-san was right before he left for China. That was six years ago. He had gone home to bid okaa-san farewell. Her frail figure, pale and bedridden with illness, brought tears to his eyes. The first thing he ought to do once the mopping-up campaigns in Nanking were over was to ask for leave to go back and see okaa-san. Otherwise, he would regret it for the rest of his life.

It had been a long day, but the bath took care of it.

After the meal, Nakamoto slumped comfortably in the sofa in the sitting room and sipped from a cup of heated sake on the end table.

Things had gone well since he entered the capital early Sunday morning. Charging into the city, hot on the heels of retreating Chinese troops, his frontline units had been overwhelmed by the sheer volume of prisoners they had taken, thousands of them, who had not even time to abandon their weapons and change into civilian clothes. It was a little inconvenient for his troops, but they had handled it satisfactorily. Since then, his troops had been carrying out mopping-up operations in the Safety Zone and in other parts of the city with great effectiveness.

At the mere thought of the Safety Zone, Nakamoto couldn't help but wonder who among his superiors had been thoughtless enough to grant legitimacy to this annoying idea. Nakamoto was certainly not willing to be bothered with having to process prisoners. Feeding them? Finding shelter for them? Getting medical treatment for their wounded? Releasing them just because they had surrendered? It was insanity.

He was pleased that his subordinates, Tajima, and others, had been able to act decisively when confronted by overwhelming numbers of prisoners. To hesitate or delay their march forward into Nanking would be to invite failure. It would be unacceptable.

Nakamoto knew of the order. He was sure all battalion commanders and their subordinates had seen it by now:

ALL PRISONERS OF WAR ARE TO BE EXECUTED.
METHOD OF EXECUTION: DIVIDE INTO GROUPS OF A
DOZEN.
SHOOT TO KILL SEPARATELY.

This order had come from Lieutenant General Asaka Yasuhiko's office. Prince Asaka Yasuhiko, the uncle of the Showa Emperor, possessed the necessary decisiveness to be a conqueror, much more so than General Matsui. Nakamoto was relieved now that Asaka was making the decisions about Nanking. Once Nanking was completely beaten, the whole of China would fall.

Nakamoto sat before the fire. As he was bathed once again in warmth, his thought drifted away.

The tinkling noise comes again, as crystal and as mysteriously titillating as he had always remembered it. The sound of undergarments rustling and dropping to the floor, followed by the sound of water splashing, lapping. Nakamoto stares at the ceiling and thinks.

Suddenly, the shoji screen moves silently to the side and Rieko walks into his room timidly in a brightly colored kimono. Her rich, lustrous dark hair is held in place high on her head to keep it out of the water. She advances toward him in small, quick steps. Already he can smell the intoxicating, sweet fragrance from her soft skin.

With impatient fingers he removes her still damp kimono and lets it fall to the floor. She is completely naked in front of him, her body covered in gooseflesh and trembling with nervous expectancy. His eyes remains focused on her while he furiously struggles to undo his own undergarments.

Rieko is lying on the floor now, a flower in bloom ready to be picked, smelled, tasted.

With a blinding fury he finds himself slathering her soft, tender face with his tongue and lips, biting her neck and touching his trembling fingers to her open mouth.

But she is different. No longer sweet, tender, or fragrant, and he is suddenly repulsed by her breath. He jerks his head away.

A limp mouth, filled with crooked, yellowed teeth, is giggling at him gleefully.

Oh God! Not that filthy, toad-like hag again!

He leaps up from the floor and runs about as if his manhood has been stung by a hornet hidden in a huge, sickly flower. Burning with rage, he runs into the next room where his Sadamitsu, *okaa-san*'s precious gift, is hanging on the wall, next to his field binoculars.

In a rage he draws his sword and a silver light flashes inside the room. He rushes back to confront the thing, but as he enters the bedroom, sword drawn, the dirty, yellow-teethed hag is nowhere to be found.

"Sir?" asks a beautiful young girl in a frightened voice. She holds a chin in one hand, her liquid eyes are fixed on the shiny tip of his sword.

He freezes.

"You're...my *mizuage* patron, remember?" she tries to give him a coy look.

"I am?"

"Yes."

"Be Still!"

"Why do you want to kill me?

"Because you're not the same anymore!"

"What?" She is confused, and terrified.

"I've paid two hundred for a pure, clean virgin that nobody has ever touched!"

"But...I was!" she stammers, trying in vain to search for the meaning in his words.

"You're not anymore!"

"But...it was you! It was you!" Her once geisha-like composure crumbles and the tears come streaming down her cheeks relentlessly. She coughs, gasping and choking on her sobs.

"You've been soiled!" He yells, standing over her, sword raised.

She cannot look at him. She reaches for the *shiromuku* to cover her body. She buries her face in it, wiping away the tears, rouge, and mucus in the soft fabric.

"My *shiromuku*!" He shrieks furiously. She's soiled the shiromuku! She's just as hopeless and despicable as those Chinese *huaguniang*!

With one perfect swing, he lets the sword fall.

Nakamoto came to half dazed. He looked around. In front of him the fire in the fireplace had grown dim, and only a few small embers crackled and spit bright orange, then faded. He heard the men upstairs talking animatedly.

He found his gold-rimmed glasses, put them on, got up, and walked upstairs to his bedroom. Zenba had prepared his bed and it was clean and neatly made.

The soldiers had just started a new song:

> You and I are cherry blossoms
>   of the same year
> Even if we're far apart

"Zenba," he called. "Tell them to shut up!"

"Yes, sir!"

He heard a door being kicked open and Zenba yelling "Quit howling, or I'll have you skinned!"

Yawning now, Nakamoto went to the bathroom one more time. Suddenly, he was aware of something cold and wet between his inner thighs.

"Zenba!" he yelled, "Prepare my bath!"

Wednesday

December 15, 1937
The Third Day

20.

"Ning-ning," Grandpa called in a low, soft voice.

Having awakened early, he had already finished his morning round of chanting. In fact, he hadn't slept much at all. He had dozed off only to wake up again the next instant . All throughout the night it was deathly quiet. He knew that something terrible had befallen Auntie Huang and her family.

Pale morning light filtered through the windows.

"Ning-ning," he called out again.

"Yes," came a muffled, sleepy voice.

"We've got to get up early."

"Why?"

"I want to go downstairs."

"Downstairs?" Ning-ning was fully awake now. "Grandpa! Did you hear anything downstairs this morning?" She asked hopefully, pushing open the lid.

"No. That's why I need to see."

"Can I come with you?"

"Only to the door," he said firmly.

Ning-ning was at his bedside now. She put her small, soft hands in his. They were very warm. Ning-ning. His only grandchild. He had to be strong for her again.

Larkie fluttered in the cage and crooned.

They both turned to look at the bird.

"Kiddo, I'll help Grandpa get up first, then take care of you. Is that okay?"

Larkie crooned again.

"How did you sleep, Ning-ning?" he asked.

"I had a bad dream," Ning-ning murmured, turning her gaze back to Grandpa.

"You did?"

"Yes." Ning-ning frowned, as if unsure whether she wanted to relive the dream by recalling it. "I was being chased by a wolf, or it could've been a lion. Anyway, it was a big, ugly animal. It was coming after me so fast, wagging its huge, bloody tongue all the time. I was so scared. I wanted to run, but my legs were heavy and I couldn't breathe. I tried to cry 'Help!' 'Help!' but nothing came out of my mouth!"

"But I heard you," he said gently.

"You did? Why didn't you come to my rescue then?"

"I did."

"How? Why didn't I see you?"

"I called your name, you mumbled something, and went back to sleep."

"Oh." There was a faraway look in Ning-ning's eyes, then she nodded and smiled.

Ning-ning helped Grandpa to his feet. With one hand on Ning-ning's shoulder, he walked slowly out of his room toward the main room.

It was a mess. The furniture was upturned and all manner of dishes, cups, plates, and all of the family's possessions lay scattered about on the floor. They navigated gingerly through the mess toward the open front door.

"My room!" Ning-ning cried out. Her quilt, pillow, clothes,

books, had all been tossed around and trampled. He could picture what it looked like inside Suo-zi's room, too. Suo-zi, his daughter, would be more than upset if she could see all this. Oh, Suo-zi, where are you now?

"It'll be all right," he murmured.

They were at the door now, peering out into the hall. He was gasping for air.

"Let me catch my breath" he said, putting his hand on the doorframe for support.

Slowly, they began to descend the stairs, one step at a time. Grandpa's legs were trembling as he took each new step, gripping the balustrade tightly with one hand and Ning-ning's shoulder with the other.

"Ning-ning," he said, stopping for air again.

"Yes?" He could hear nervousness in her voice.

"Remember what I said? You stay outside till I call you."

Ning-ning nodded.

They were at the open door now. They stood, waiting, not daring to breathe. Grandpa took his hand from Ning-ning's shoulder and braced himself in the doorframe.

He began to feel his way in, alone, slowly, trembling with each step. He reached out to a nearby chair.

The body of Uncle Huang, partially obscured by the chair, lay on his back on the floor. There was a large bullet hole right in the middle of his chest. Had they shot him when the kicked open the door or as they left?

Grandpa paused a moment and looked up. Two bare legs dangled from the edge of a nearby bed. For lack of space, the twins' bed had been put in the living room. Grandpa couldn't see the rest of the body. It was covered with a quilt and a mosquito net that was left hanging from the ceiling even during winter, but the quilt and net were splattered with blood. He took a couple of small steps. Near the foot of the bed was Ermei's body, naked from the waist down. There were several deep stab wounds in her belly and all along her thighs. She lay in a dark purple circle of blood which formed a halo around her lifeless body.

Auntie Huang's body was completely naked and tied to a chair. A long, bloodstained knife was thrust into the chair right between her outspread legs. Her head, nearly severed, dangled disgustingly, held to her body only by a few stubborn threads of flesh and sinew. On her blue-black right temple, still visible, was a sickening gunshot wound.

Grandpa closed his eyes tightly. He struggled to stand, using his remaining strength to stifle the nauseating dizziness fomenting in the pit of his stomach.

Tears streamed down Grandpa's face.

You've got to be strong, you've got to be strong, he reminded himself.

He turned his head back to the door and caught Ning-ning's head peeping in.

"No!" he shouted angrily. "Stay outside!"

She started to sob.

"I'm sorry," he said in a much softer tone.

Ning-ning burst out crying.

"It's too horrible for your eyes, you know," he sighed, breathing laboriously.

"Ning-ning," he said.

"Yes," came the sobbing, tearful answer.

"Can you get a few things for me?"

"What?"

"Incense sticks, straw paper, and some linens?"

Ning-ning nodded.

"You know where to find them?

She nodded again.

Feeling his way slowly along the wall back to the door, he could hear Ning-ning's footsteps hurrying upstairs. A few moments later, she came running back down.

"They've messed up Mama's room, too," Ning-ning said when she was back, her eyes glistening with tears.

"I know, " he sighed. "It'll be all right."

Ning-ning had also brought something very special: her baby quilt, the one her mama had made with her own hands. She handed it to Grandpa.

Grandpa took it and studied it carefully, unsure of what to do.

"I want Da-mei and Er-mei to have it," she said, heaving with sobs.

He put all the linens on his shoulders and everything else in his pockets, and felt his way back in to the room. Ning-ning lingered by the door frame but did not go in.

He couldn't look at her: Yun-lian, Auntie Huang. She was like a daughter to him. Tears flowed down his creased face once more as he grasped at the knife's handle, gripped it feebly, then shaking and quivering uncontrollably as he struggled to pull it out of the wooden chair. He jerked back as the knife came free, then he dropped it on the floor. He took out a large white sheet, unfolded it, then covered her head and body.

"Go back to sleep now," he sobbed.

"Grandpa?" Ning-ning called.

"Yes?"

"Can I help you?"

"Not yet. Wait till I call you."

He moved over to the girls now. Every time they saw him, the twins would greet him as if he were their own Grandpa. Da-mei, Er-mei, and Ning-ning had played together like they were all sisters. He took Ning-ning's baby quilt and spread it over Er-mei's body. He turned to Da-mei and touched the quilt under which her body lay.

With another sheet he covered Uncle Huang last. Then he called for Ning-ning.

She walked into the room, slowly. She tried to keep her eyes focused on Grandpa but she looked quickly around the room, allowing her gaze to fall upon the floor, the bed, the chair. Grandpa opened his arms and she ran into them. They cried together.

"OK, let's set this up," he said, drying his eyes with his sleeve.

He took out the incense sticks, and tried to light them with a match, but his hands shook uncontrollably.

"Let me try." Ning-ning took the sticks and lit them. As thin wisps of grey smoke curled upwards, she put the glowing sticks into a small glass bottle and placed it in the middle of the room.

Ning-ning had also found a small bowl and a dry steamed bun. She put the bun in the bowl and placed it next to the incense sticks.

Next, Ning-ning lit a small handful of yellowish straw paper and placed it before the incense sticks and the steamed bun. A tiny flame flickered at a corner of the paper, and soon it had caught fire, burning with a crisp yellow flame.

"May they have food in the next world," Grandpa began to chant, his soft voice quivering. "May they have money to spend in their next lives. May there be no war, no violence, no hatred, no greed, no misery in the next world and in this world and in all the worlds here and beyond...."

Ning-ning was murmuring along with him, her hands folded in front of her like a little Buddha.

A few moments later they turned to leave, shuffling out of the room slowly. Upstairs, their home was flooded with sunlight when Grandpa slowly got back into bed again, his breath coming in gasps. Ning-ning crawled back into the coffin.

"Grandpa?" she called.

"Yes?"

"Why do the Japanese come all the way here to kill people?"

"Because they wanted something here."

"Like what?"

"Like...mountains, rivers, land, air, everything perhaps."

"Don't they have all of that back home?"

"Yes, but they want more."

"That's too greedy. If they really need more, they could have come and borrowed some, like neighbors, but they don't have to kill, right?"

"They don't want to borrow. They want to take from their neighbors whatever they want and they want so much."

"Grandpa," Ning-ning said, after a pause, "Do you think they will get away with it?"

"They'll repent one day. True repentance is their only hope for salvation."

"What's repentance, Grandpa?"

"Well...it's hard to explain." He thought for a second. "You want to hear a story?"

"I'm always ready for stories."

About fifteen hundred years ago, he began, Nanking was the capital of a small dynasty called Liang. There was an emperor, Wudi, and an empress, whose name was Xi-xi. The empress was beautiful, intelligent, and very good at calligraphy and needlework. Wudi was very fond of her. However, Xi-xi suffered from one flaw: She was prone to fits of extreme jealousy, which drove her to lash out at people viciously. When the court's chief monk became the latest victim of Xi-xi's vicious tongue, Wudi gave her a dressing-down in front of everybody else in the court. Consumed by anger and shame, Xi-xi threw herself into a deep well in the garden.

"Killing herself just for that?" Ning-ning sounded incredulous.

"I know."

After Xi-xi's death, Wudi was tortured by a sense of guilt every day. He felt so bad about having caused Xi-xi's death that he tossed and turned in bed every night and couldn't get one wink of sleep.

One night, as he sat in his chamber drowsing fitfully, Wudi heard crickets chirping in the corner. Opening his eyes, he saw a huge snake coiled not far from where he was.

"Oh, my!" Ning-ning exclaimed.

Wudi was terrified, too, but there was nowhere to run. Desperate, he jumped on to a table and said:

"The court is tightly guarded and it's no place for you. Why are you here? Do you want to hurt me?"

"No," the snake said softly. "Please do not be frightened by this ugly body of mine. In fact, I was your empress in my former life, but my viciousness has imprisoned me in this hideous form as punishment. Now, except for the deep well in the garden, I have no place to go, no food to eat, and I'm plagued by venomous insects biting me every day. My suffering has made me think of all the offences I have committed and I repent from the bottom of my heart. But I don't know how to show to the world that I have repented. Then I thought about your loving kindness to me during my former life, so here I'm in front of you to beseech you to help me."

"Poor Xi-xi," Ning-ning sighed.

Wudi sighed, too, but once he rubbed his eyes and looked again, the snake was gone.

The next morning, Wudi gathered all the Buddhist monks in court and asked them what to do to help Xi-xi find salvation.

"The only salvation is in genuine repentance," all the monks said, but they left the details for Wudi to figure out for himself.

Wudi began to devote himself to studying Buddhist scriptures. Eventually he was able to write ten thick volumes on the definition of repentance, asking Lord Buddha to pardon both Xi-xi and himself for their failures. To further prove his sincerity, he established a new temple and appointed Xi-xi, or her ghost, to be in charge of sacrificial rituals. In the end, he became more benevolent to his subjects. Under his rule, Nanking prospered and people were quite happy.

"Wudi," said Ning-ning, "he really meant to show repentance!"

Grandpa nodded and continued. Years later, one summer night, as he was drowsing again in his chamber, Wudi was awakened by a wholesome, refreshing fragrance. He felt as if his own soul had been cleansed. Opening his eyes, he saw, to his joy, a beautiful lady in front of him. The lady bowed deeply and said:

"I'm the reincarnation of the snake you saw a long time ago. Your loving kindness has saved me and I'm here to thank you."

The beautiful lady gave another deep bow and in the blink of an eye she was gone. Thus, Wudi and Xi-xi showed true repentance, and both have been rewarded with salvation.

"What happens after that?" Ning-ning asked.

"After that? The end."

They were both quiet for a while.

"Those Japanese," Ning-ning said, as if wondering aloud, "who killed Auntie Huang's family, can they find salvation?

"If they're truly repentant. Yes."

"But, what they did...it's a thousand times worse than being jealous or having a vicious tongue." Ning-ning scowled.

"Yes, it's worse. But, if they're truly repentant, there's still hope."

21.

He had to behave differently today.

That was Brigadier General Nakamoto's order. The international prestige of the Empire of the Rising Sun was at stake, the general had warned sternly.

Tajima knew very little about this college other than that it was an all-women's college. Would all the young women still be there? That would not be possible, he thought, with the war, the mopping-up campaigns, and everything else going on, but he was hoping that not all had fled in advance of the victorious Japanese army. After all, this college was now the refugee center for women and children. That would make his side assignment from Nakamoto a bit easier.

Half an hour's march brought Tajima and his troops right outside the front gate of the college.

The machine-gun platoon began to position themselves right away: A machine-gun was mounted at the main entrance, and the others atop the walls and the side gates.

The guard, a middle-aged Chinese, rushed up to Second Lieutenant Kuroda, who was at the head of Tajima's procession.

"Sir, this is a Safety Zone!" the guard exclaimed.

Kuroda slapped him hard across the face.

Tajima was pleased. Kuroda had not hesitated at all.

"To hell with your Safety Zone! We are here to search for

soldiers," Kuroda pushed the guard aside.

Tajima and his troops, over a hundred of them, marched in through the gate.

He surveyed the scene. The buildings were quite impressive with their upturned eaves and grand columns, not unlike many buildings he had seen back in Kyoto, Osaka, or Tokyo.

He had to be on his best behavior today. After all, this college was run by Americans and he didn't want to disgrace the empire.

A tall, middle-aged American woman, along with a group of Chinese, all respectably dressed, was walking toward him. She had to be that American woman he had been briefed about earlier. She was almost a full head taller than him.

He bowed. "How do you do, Madame," he said, extending his hand to the American woman, when the two groups met in the middle of the road. "I am Lieutenant Colonel Tajima of the Imperial Japanese Army."

Lieutenant Fujii, who had gone to missionary schools back in Japan, acted as interpreter.

"How do you do, sir," the American woman replied, shaking his hand. "I'm Professor Vautrin, acting dean of Ginling College for Women. What can I do for you?"

"We are searching for Chinese troops who could be hiding in the buildings here." Tajima explained.

"This is a refugee center for women and children," explained Professor Vautrin, "I can assure you that there are no soldiers here."

She was looking right into his face when she spoke, and looking down at him as well. Tajima had never encountered this before and felt compelled to puff out his chest a bit more than usual. There was only the slightest awkward pause, but then Tajima composed himself, as the American woman was waiting for a response.

"I don't distrust what you have said at all, Madame," he said. "However, I am still obligated to check with our own eyes and report back to my superiors."

"Sir, with all due respect, your troops have been coming in at least ten to twenty times a day for the last two days!"

"Oh?" he feigned ignorance, "they must have been from other units. My orders are to ensure—"

"If you insist, sir," the American woman merely shrugged.

Tajima walked alongside the American woman when the inspection tour began. They were followed by several dozen of junior officers and soldiers and a few of the college's staff members. Tajima noticed that Zenba, Nakamoto's orderly, was right behind him.

As they walked across the quad, Tajima noticed that almost every tree branch was bending with the weight of women's and children's clothes hung out to dry.

They pushed open a heavy wooden door in the Science Hall and stepped into a large room. The sense of space was immense, and the weight of the air in the room seemed to bring a sense of silence to all who entered. Their footsteps echoed on the hardwood floor, but for Tajima it was an eerie feeling. At the far end of the hall, on an altar, was a statue of Jesus on the Cross. Tajima had seen that image before.

In the front of the room, close to the altar, were a group of women, some middle-aged, some quite young, all sitting in a circle on the floor. Each held an open book on her lap. At the sight of the soldiers, they stood up in alarm, but the tall American woman motioned for them to remain calm.

"What are they doing here?" Tajima asked.

"Reading the Bible and praying," replied the American woman.

"Praying? For what?" He was puzzled.

"For peace."

He turned to look at her. This American woman. Had she just mocked him? There was no sarcasm in her eyes. The tensed muscles in his face relaxed.

"Yes, for peace," he mumbled.

Tajima turned to leave, but a young girl sitting close to the altar caught his eye. There was something about her which set her apart from everyone else. She looked to be about thirteen or fourteen. Tajima could see that she was beautiful of course, but she seemed so absorbed in her reading that it was as if he did not even exist. He felt piqued.

"What's that you're reading?" he walked closer to her and asked.

The girl looked up, as if just being awakened from her reverie.

"You mean me?"

Her eyes were large and liquid. Perfect. Pure.

"I'm trying to understand something," the girl murmured, pointing at a page in the book she was reading. "Here, Jesus says, 'I say to you, Love your enemies and pray for those who persecute you, so that you may be children of your Father in heaven.'"

Fujii tried to translate the passage for him, but Tajima merely furrowed his eyebrows in confusion and shook his head.

"That's what I want to understand," the girl murmured, a

puzzled look in her large eyes. She turned to look at the tall American woman, "Loving your enemies? Praying for them? That must be very hard."

The American woman smiled warmly, and said, "It is very hard, but a true Christian should do exactly that. Jesus makes the sun rise on the evil and on the good; He sends rain on the righteous and on the...."

Fujii was about to interpret again, but Tajima waved him off. Instead, he gave Zenba a meaningful look.

Zenba nodded.

This girl would be perfect for Nakamoto.

After another half-hour, their inspection had concluded. They had found no Chinese soldiers. Tajima gladly signed his name to a document provided to him by the American women, in essence declaring that the college had been searched. That would be the end of it. As he shook hands with the American woman one last time before turning to leave, Tajima puffed out his chest once again and proceeded to lead his troops out of the campus.

22.

Early in the afternoon, Helen returned to her room in Lavender Hall, one of the dormitories on South Hill.

"You've got to take good care of yourself," Professor Vautrin had insisted, and she obeyed, like a good, dutiful daughter.

Helen dropped onto the bed, stretched out, and breathed long and deep. She had been up since the early morning, assisting groups of new refugees in settling down within the campus. She had devised simple organizational games for women and children, and had hugged and embraced dozens of young girls who had been ravaged by the Japanese soldiers.

She was three months into her pregnancy. Even up to now, Helen hadn't experienced any serious, upsetting physical reactions except for the occasional morning sickness. Jane, a friend of hers who had graduated two years earlier and married a year ago, had had such a terrible time coping with her pregnancy. Jane would throw up so hard, doubling up as the nausea hit her as if she would choke to death at any time. Only after the fifth month or so did her condition seem to stabilize.

Why was it that she was so lucky? Was it because she worked so hard? More than that, Helen mused. Growing up, she had been a tomboy: climbing tress, doing cartwheels. Her parents didn't believe in girls growing up like the character of Daiyu in *A Dream of Red Mansions*: that weak, almost tragically sick kind of feminine beauty so many young girls had loved to emulate. She had enjoyed all the girlish games, but her athleticism and rough and tumble nature had persisted well into her adolescence.

"Look at your daughter, Hui-ping," the aunties and grannies in the neighborhood would all say to her mother, "Who would want to marry her when she grows up? She's so wild!"

Her mother would smile knowingly, "She'll probably just stay with us and take care of me and Yao-guang when we get old, and not her in-laws."

So much for tradition. Who wants to marry some dim-witted boy and be a slave for his parents anyway!

While a student at Ginling, Helen's academic interests had flowered. She had decided to major in education but was also interested in social work, and was equally strong in English, Mathematics, Chinese, History, and Social Sciences. Also unusual was the way she would always look forward to the physical education classes with an enthusiasm that was very rare among her schoolmates.

She was quite an accomplished athlete when it came to volleyball, badminton, and basketball. Though not particularly tall or strong, she was known for her quickness and agility. During her senior year, she was captain of the basketball team and led her teammates to a hard-fought victory over the faculty team.

Her room at the college was small with very little furniture and minimal decorations. As a student she used to share a room with three other classmates, and there was always something to talk about. When she graduated with honors five months ago, she was invited to teach at the Homecraft School. Now, she had a room all to herself. Even though she enjoyed the privacy she now had, Helen missed the camaraderie of her roommates and remembered those days with fondness.

A single wooden bed nestled against the right side wall. Upon it was the handcrafted quilt of red, yellow, and blue—a gift from her mother. On one corner of the bed was a cupid doll. For a sewing project while she was still in middle school, she was supposed to make dresses for this cute little doll with a porcelain head and curly golden hair. She had managed to make a jacket that more or less fit, but she was having a hard time trying to come up with a pair of matching trousers.

"Why don't you try a skirt ?" Her father had suggested.

She loved the idea and went about designing and making the skirt. The result was something bold and simple: a bell-shaped bag with both ends wide open. Dressed in those mismatched jacket and skirt, her doll must have been the oddest-looking Cupid in the world. To her little brother Dong-zi, at least, it certainly was.

Dong-zi had laughed hysterically at the sight of the strange foreign doll, reached out to grab it, but instead knocked it to the floor by mistake. A crack across the doll's forehead was still visible despite the tresses of rich blond hair dangling there.

Right by the window was a three-legged writing desk with an antique-looking reading lamp that hadn't been used for about a week now. On a small table next to the bed was a framed wedding photograph-she in her white wedding gown, more demure in appearance than her usual self, smiling warmly; and Peng-fei, the bridegroom, in a dark suit and tie, tall, handsome, grinning bashfully.

On the facing walls were three scrolls painted by her father in watercolor: flaming plum blossoms in early spring; tall, sturdy, yet delicate bamboo stalks caught in a winter gale; and a pink and white lotus flower solemnly in bloom upon a still grey pond which reflected the misty grey sky, awaiting the rain.

Small as it was, her room contained almost everything Helen felt she really needed. Even Peng-fei, who had such a passion for the vast, endless spaces in the sky, hadn't complained about experiencing anything close to claustrophobia here. After all, he had already gotten used to being strapped in the tiny space of the plane's cockpit. They hadn't even talked about when or where to find a place to settle down when all this was over. They hadn't had the time. Even their wedding had been rushed.

That was early August, when the Japanese warplanes began to fly bombing missions over Nanking. Reverend John Magee had just begun to say "Dearly beloved, we are gathered here today at our Episcopal Church in the sight of God" when a heart-piercing siren wailed into the sky outside. There was a hushed commotion among the gathering of about a hundred family members and guests: Helen's parents and brother, Peng-fei's brother-the best man-and his friends from the air corps, Professor Vautrin, and a number of other professors and friends from Ginling College. The pastor paused for an imperceptible second and continued: "to join this man, Peng-fei Yang, and this woman, Helen Chuan Ling, in holy matrimony."

When it was time for the groom to kiss the bride, the siren was still wailing away. There was a commotion coming from the streets outside. Some of the guests toward the back of the church had already left.

"I'll make it up to you," Peng-fei whispered in her ear after planting a quick kiss on her lips. She blushed profusely.

Tall, handsome, and a captain in the newly established air

corps, Peng-fei had been the Prince Charming that frequented the dreams of many young women in Nanking. The boldest among them showered him with letters with their own photographs enclosed. Peng-fei had been flattered, but didn't let that kind of attention go to his head. He waited and bided his time until he had spotted her at a dance party at the University of Nanking.

She hadn't gone to such parties often and she wasn't the prettiest that Saturday evening: she was dressed in a simple short-sleeved white blouse and a black skirt, just like a typical female college student. And yet, Peng-fei later told her, there was something about her, a kind of quiet, yet sunny vivaciousness—which reflected neither the traditional Chinese girl's timidity nor the overly modernized woman's aggressiveness—that had attracted him irresistibly. And that was the beginning of a yearlong courtship.

"You're just saying this to please me, aren't you?" Helen had teased.

"You want me to swear?"

The young captain raised his right hand and said solemnly,

"If I have lied let me be hit by the Five Thunders of Heaven..." but Helen abruptly covered his mouth with her palm.

"Okay, I believe you," she giggled happily.

Peng-fei was not exactly the kind of Prince Charming Helen had been dreaming of. Busy with volunteering at the Homecraft School for girls from poor families in the community, following her sports and other interests as well as trying to stay on top of so many reading assignments from her professors, she hadn't had much time to form a clear picture of her Prince Charming. Someone she would love to marry and to start a family of her own. That was all still too far away for her. And a young army officer was perhaps the furthest from her mind. So, when she fell in love with Peng-fei it was a gradual, slow tumble rather than a quick, precipitous plunge. Even her father, open-minded as he was, had cautioned her about a life with a military man in such troubled times.

"See how much your mother has had to put up with me?" the colonel had said, while walking with Helen and her mother around Ginling campus one day.

"But she is a very happy woman!" Helen had retorted. "Right, mom?"

"Oh, yes!" her mother replied, "I wouldn't trade him for anybody else in the whole world."

The three of them had laughed.

Helen lay on the bed and sighed. She turned on her side and pulled out something from under her pillow: a small diary. She had been keeping a diary-on and off-since her middle school days. It was an old book, full of memories. She did not write in it regularly, but only when the occasion struck her. When she was unusually busy, she would often forget about it for weeks at a time.

She open it and flipped through the pages. She stopped at the entry she wrote two years ago: when she returned to Ginling after a three-week winter break.

Feb. 20
While the handkerchiefs were still waving "farewells" to Mom and Dong-zi (Dad was in Shanghai), the unkind train sped along steadily toward Nanking. Traveling has always been exciting to

me but I have always dreaded bidding farewell to homefolk. It is always such a heavy heart event. At five o'clock we were finally at the journey's end, out of the carriage, and within the college walls.

Stepping into the dorm, I found a pile of letters waiting on my desk. At suppertime familiar faces met each other with mirth and friendliness. Bath taken and bed made, I threw myself drowsily down, the stillness of the room seemed to have sympathy with me....

Helen read her awkward prose. Her English had improved so much since then. She turned to the next entry.

Feb. 22

My alarm clock woke me early. A solemn stillness reigned over the dormitory-"Autumn Sound Hall." The rest of the girls were still in bed. The birds singing gaily gave me peace of mind. I rose immediately, washed and dressed. At seven o'clock I took a morning walk up on the hill to enjoy a deep intake of morning air. The misty Purple Mountain to the east was basking in the radiant glory of a rising sun, the charm from the skies seemed to melt my soul though this appearance is unseen and unrevealed.

The first chapel was conducted by the president, and the dean. The classes were running on schedule. I turned over the new leaf of my schoolwork with this motto for my guide:
"Whatever I have tried to do in life,
I have tried with all my heart to do well;
Whatever I have devoted myself to
I have devoted myself completely to,
In great aims and in small
I have always been thoroughly in earnest."

She smiled at the thought and her own spontaneity in composing this entry. She turned a couple of blank pages and found the next entry:

March 25

The birds are chirping in the trees and bushes and spring seems to be well on her way. It is the time for our youth of feeling to shout out to the youth of nature: Welcome!

The birds seem to favor our Ginling campus. In a few more days or weeks, perhaps, magpies will be here making their rough-stick nests on the top of campus buildings. I saw quite a few of such nests on the top of the Science Hall and the Central Hall last spring. Folks say magpies bring good, auspicious tidings to you when they sing on your treetops. Will they be bringing any more tidings of joy to us, to Ginling this spring? Haven't lots of good things happened to us already?

I have also seen doves or pigeons (what's the difference, anyway?) twittering on top of one of the buildings or flying overhead. Before I read the Bible, I didn't know they were in any way special, but now, whenever I see them, I feel a kind of joy that words fail to describe.

And speaking of joy, I have to mention the skylark. It is small, almost dark, and plainly dressed, but blessed with a sweet, clear note which it utters while soaring into the sky. I have seen a few on the hill in the campus. We Chinese sometimes call it "the messenger of heaven," because its singing is so heavenly. And what did Shelley say about the skylark? Oh, I'll have to look it up later, something about the bird being a "blithe Spirit," "a cloud of fire," or "a star of Heaven?" Isn't that something!

She re-read her prose. It seemed to leap up in bursts of energy.

She flipped through more entries. She read her complaints of having too many assignments from professors ("who don't mind whether I have time to study or not but they like to give quizzes almost every day") and of her club and social responsibilities on campus, and so on. There were Christmas and New Year's parties, and her social studies project. It was while working on this project that she had met Eva and Ning-ning.

The two girls were much younger than she. When the three of them stood together, they were like do-re-fa rather than do-re-mi. Eva, in particular, was quite mature for her age, but then again she had suffered more than most in her short life. There was always a melancholy look in her eyes, and an airy, almost otherworldly aura around her. Ning-ning, on the other hand, had a cheerful, sunny temperament. Even though she had seen Ning-ning no more than five or six times, Helen felt like she had known her all her life. In many ways, Ning-ning was almost an exact copy of herself seven or eight years ago.

The last time Eva had brought Ning-ning to the campus, several of the faculty and staff who saw them all together had remarked aloud:

"Are they your sisters?"

"Of course!" Helen had replied proudly, a wide smile on her face.

Eva was now at the refugee center on campus. They still saw each other from time to time.

But what about Ning-ning? Helen hadn't heard anything about Ning-ning recently and she had not come to the refugee center.

A sudden noise startled Helen out of her recollection. A thumping sound came from far down the hallway and footsteps could be heard on the wooden floorboards as people ran outside. Helen bolted up and opened the door.

There was a scream, then some shouting and yelling. Helen found her heart beating furiously. She rushed down the hallway and ran outside.

A small crowd of people had gathered outside the hall. In the distance Helen could see two Japanese soldiers struggling to carry off a girl. They were already at the side gate of the campus.

"What's happened?" she asked, breathlessly.

"They've taken Eva!" came the reply.

23.

Eva had never seen a bathtub so big, white, and shiny, filled with so much crystal clear, hot water.

The tub's snow-white porcelain surface was cool to the touch, but standing alongside she could feel the intense heat as the steam rose, covering the white tiles and silver fixtures in warm, moist vapor.

Eva began to disrobe, slowly, drowsily, almost as if in a trance. She stepped gingerly into the tub, one leg at a time. Her upper body shivered, and instinctively she knelt closer to the water's surface. She touched the water with her fingertips, made a few slow, small circles, and, cupping the hot water in her hand, let it run down her shoulders.

Slowly, she crouched down and closed her eyes. The water rose and lapped at the rim of the tub. She could feel the water's gentle yet persistent buoyancy. Its heat penetrated her skin from chin down to toe. She seemed to float.

Eva rested her head against the edge of the tub and lay there. How did she get here? The events of the afternoon were little more than a blur. She remembered reading from the Bible in the science hall chapel when a group of Japanese soldiers came in.

She found reading the Bible to be quite difficult. Certainly the English was not something she was used to, having only started to learn to read it some two years ago. Admittedly, she was fascinated by the stories of Adam and Eve in the Garden of Eden, Noah and the Ark, the brothers Abel and Cain, and others, but once she started to learn about Jesus she had to think about it harder. What did his words mean: Love your enemy so that you could be God's children.

She had puzzled over it, and that was why she was nearly oblivious to the commotion in the chapel as the soldiers walked in.

Now she remembered. When the soldiers had left and she rose to go to the restroom in the hallway, she noticed two of them still loitering outside the chapel. They seemed to be examining the colorful flyers posted in the hallway. She saw a short, squat man gesturing her to come over, almost as if he wanted her to explain something to him that he had seen but didn't understand. Cautiously, she did so, but even when she stood more than an arm's length away, he reached out like a striking snake and caught her arm, wrapping his other arm around her waist with lightning quickness. She hadn't even had time to react as a thick, calloused hand was placed over her mouth. She flailed her arms and tried to kick, but the other solider hurried over to subdue her. She was too small and too weak to fend off her attackers: a baby rabbit caught by two ravenous wolves. They were carrying her outside now, across the campus. She remembered someone screaming hysterically and other cries of alarm from those she passed. But no one intervened. How could they? Her near weightless body had been carried off so easily.

Eva plunged her head into the steamy warm water and began to scrub her hair, working her fingers deep into her scalp and the thin black strands curled around her hands.

She wondered if she would just disappear, just like her

parents.

They had left when she was about eight and never came home. That was just over six years ago. They owned a small goods store. Indeed, Eva's early childhood memories were filled with sights and smells of small, wooden containers displaying all kinds of dried and preserved dates, walnuts, chestnuts, acorn nuts, black mushrooms, and all manner of herbs.

One or twice a year, Papa would spend a few weeks traveling to Manchuria in the northeast tip of China. When he returned he carried bags and bags of new goods to sell. People in Nanking loved such products for the nourishing properties and medicinal virtue. Her parents were not rich, but they worked hard to keep the store running and worrying about their next meal was never a problem.

It was in early September that Papa decided to take Mama with him on one of these regular trips north. Mama had never seen that part of China before. They had arranged for their neighbor to assist Granny and Eva in helping to take care of the store while they were away.

She did go as far as the Lower Pass Dock train station, together with Granny, to see them off. It was the first time Mama was really going anywhere, and she was excited, giggling with girlish excitement at the prospect. As the train started to build up steam and puffed and chugged, Mama waved to her and Granny. Soon, Papa's head appeared at the window, too, grinning happily and waving. He seemed so happy it was like he was waving to everyone on the platform. A minute later, the train pulled out of the station. Her eyes followed the train, and she could still see Mama's red and white patterned handkerchief fluttering, lingering briefly outside the window.

Life in the store went on as before, with all the regular customers coming by and asking about Papa and Mama's trip. Even when one full month had passed and Papa and Mama hadn't returned, Granny told Eva not to worry. China was a big country and it took time to get from one place to the other. When October had passed into November, she could see the anxious look on Granny's face. Waiting. Waiting. November waned and the first snow started to fall in mid-December, but still her parents had not come home. Granny turned and mumbled in her sleep, but Eva was awake. Every little sound she heard made her sit up in bed, so convinced was she that it was her parents coming through the front door, but at last she drifted off, only to wake up each morning to an empty house.

Granny would be sitting at the door, crying, sighing, and crying some more, in the days and months afterward. Eva was afraid she would go blind from all her crying and sobbing. By now even Eva had heard that the Japanese army had flooded into Mukden, a city in Manchuria. China had been invaded. Eventually, they closed the store and sold off everything in it in order to support themselves.

Sometimes she wondered if it was punishment for her failure to bring in any little brothers. Her Chinese name, which she seldom now used, was, after all, "Zhao-di," which meant, "beckoning brothers." Perhaps her parents had been disappointed with their firstborn being a daughter. They must have wanted a son badly.

One early summer afternoon four years ago, when she went to buy salt, soy sauce, and straw paper at a small store on Shaanxi Road, she saw a girl, a bit younger than she walking toward her. When they got close enough, the girl gave her a faint smile and

Eva smiled back awkwardly. The girl had two neat, radiant braids that almost touched her shoulders as she walked. She was wearing the same kind of school uniform that Eva used to wear, with a small schoolbag dangling at her hip. Why hadn't she seen the girl before?

When Eva bumped into the girl again a few days later along the same street and when they smiled at each other again, they opened their mouths to say something almost simultaneously. Then they giggled.

The girl said her name was Ning-ning, and that she lived close by. Eva's home was close to Shaanxi Road, which was connected to Ninghai Road and Sun Yat-sen Boulevard North. Ning-ning lived in one of those small winding alleys toward the other end of the same side street.

They became very good friends and Eva had gotten to know Ning-ning's family: her mother, father, and her grandpa. Whenever she visited she was warmly welcomed.

One early spring morning two years ago, two female students from Ginling College knocked on Eva's door. They were offering basic schooling to girls in poor families free of charge. Eva was 12 then. She desperately wanted to go to school.

"No!" Granny had mumbled stubbornly, rocking slowly in her squeaky chair. "What good will come out of girls going to school?"

But the two young women talked Granny into changing her mind. The education would be free, they said. It was an all-girls school and in a building inside a walled compound of an all-women's college, so she would be safe. They convinced Granny that all girls needed to prepare themselves for the future.

Granny mumbled something again and nodded. Eva didn't

hate Granny. That was only what she had known all her life: that girls had no use for books, and so on. In the years since her parents had disappeared, Eva now wondered whether Granny had come to blame her mother for whatever had happened to her father, Granny's son:

"Girls and women are not only useless," she could hear Granny's weary voice croaking, "they can bring trouble, too."

One of the two Ginling students who had visited her that day was Miss Ling, but she liked to be called Helen. Eva thought she was beautiful, with a cheerful, sunny personality and joyous confidence. She had admired Helen from the first time she saw her. Helen even asked her mother to send some of her old clothes for Eva to wear. Most importantly, it was Helen who had helped Eva choose her English name:

"Somehow...you're Eva," Helen had "...and Eva is you!"

From then on she ceased to be known as Zhao-di.

Eva loved the sound of her new name. She had become a new person and for the first time in many years she felt a sense of hope.

There was a large, framed mirror above the porcelain sink in the bathroom. The mirror was covered with steam. Eva reached for a white towel and began to dry herself. With her hand she wiped the mirror clear.

She had never seen herself naked like this before. She looked at her eyes. They were unusually large and deep, but behind them even she could see there lay a pensive sadness that welled up from someplace deep inside. Her nose was straight and delicate, her lips the color of fresh cherries, and her cheeks were soft and the color of a pink-white rose.

She had grown and matured in the years since her parents disappeared. Her skin was soft and smooth. Her breasts had grown into firm, delicate mounds with rosy-red buds at their center. She could see how small her waist was, as well as the pronounced curvature of her hips, which must have been what made people-men and adolescent boys especially-start to look at her more intently wherever she walked.

She was no longer the little girl she used to be any longer. She remembered again the first time she saw a patch of red in her underwear. She was terrified and ran all the way to Ginling College.

"It means you're a little woman now," Helen had said with a kind, mysterious smile on her face. Everything had been alright after that, and since that day Eva had been watching her burgeoning womanhood with curiosity, pride, and a lingering sense of worry.

Miss Hua, the tall, distinguished-looking American professor, had come to the Homecraft School a few times, too. She had even taught a lesson there. She talked about why girls should be as valuable as boys in society, why girls should feel proud of themselves, and why girls were as much entitled to a decent education as anybody else.

"It's because," Miss Hua said at the conclusion of her lesson, "God, our Father, loves you not a bit less than He does the boys."

Eva didn't know if she had understood everything Miss Hua was saying about God, but she felt that she had understood. As she started to learn more it awakened within her an intriguing sense of wonder. Once the bombing had started, Eva read and re-read the Bible every day, even as refugees began to pour into the campus. She had waited for Granny to arrive, but when she learned that Granny had died in the bombing, she experienced a surprising, profound sense of peace.

Eva had been shown a few pieces of clothing arranged in a neat pile on a chair next to the bathtub, and had told to put them on after bathing. A small comb also lay on top of the pile. She picked up the first item of clothing and unfolded it. It was a long, cream-colored under robe of some sort. It was made of a wondrously soft material she had never seen before. She put it on. It was cool against her skin and reached down to her knees. There was also a small white sash which she used to tie the robe around her waist.

The next article of clothing was a large robe. It was thick but soft, and light blue in color, with intricate designs of billowing clouds, cherry blossoms, and maple leaves. The sleeves were large and when she put it on it reached to her ankles. She tied the robe around her waist with another sash.

On the bottom of the pile was a pair of sandals with thick, red velvet straps. They felt cold and hard when she slid her feet in.

She looked at herself in the mirror again. Suddenly, she felt her heart beat faster. She reached for the comb and started to run it slowly through her short hair. Then, she turned, and, with a few cautious steps, slowly made her way out of the bathroom.

24.

It was completely dark inside now.

The night was quiet. Ning-ning had settled into her hideout once more. The lid was half-open, propped up by the umbrella. Her eyes stared out into the darkness.

Grandpa could not sleep. He merely drifted in and out of consciousness. He was not floating airily, as if being carried by a cloud in the sky, but merely hovering on fog creeping close to the ground. Any sound would bring his feet crashing to earth.

The scene downstairs was still very much on his mind. Uncle Huang, Auntie Huang, Da-mei and Er-mei. They were still there, covered but without proper burial. They could not rest in peace, and their spirits would be restless. Yet, who could give them a proper burial? He and Ning-ning had done what little they could, but it was not enough.

The Huangs were gone, just like the Lius before them at the corner store.

"Grandpa?" Ning-ning's voice interrupted his thought.

"Yes?"

"I have been thinking of what you said about repentance today."

"Mmm Hmm." Grandpa mumbled softly.

"Is that the reason why you chant everyday?"

"You mean if I am repenting for my wrongdoings by chanting everyday?"

"Well..." Ning-ning stuttered awkwardly.

"Yes," he said, "that's exactly what I'm doing: repenting for my wrongdoings."

"But how could you have committed any wrongdoings? You're afraid to step on an ant."

"But I may have stepped on a few ants without even knowing it."

"What does that mean?"

"It means that I had done many things before I became a Buddhist. Before I became a vegetarian."

"But they weren't bad things, right?"

"It's still a wrongdoing for me any way you look at it."

"Oh." Ning-ning said in a resigned tone. "What made you become a Buddhist?"

"Life." he offered.

"Life?"

"There's too much suffering in life."

"You mean things like the war?" He could hear tremors in her voice. "Like Auntie Huang, and everyone dying?"

"That's right."

"What else?" Ning-ning persisted.

"I mean there had been lots of suffering even before the war started, and even before I was born."

"Before you were even born?"

"Yes," he sighed. "It's a long story. Want to hear it?"

"Mmm Hmm." Came the enthusiastic response.

The Jins had been living in Nanking for many, many generations. They could be traced back to at least the reign of the Hongwu Emperor over six hundred years ago. Some of the

Jins must have been drafted during the Hongwu Emperor's campaign to expand the city walls. Even though the city had experienced periods of prosperity and decline, peace and conflict, it met its worst fate during the uprising started by one man named Hong Xiuquan over eighty years ago.

Hong was an ambitious young man who had failed to pass the government examinations several times. You can imagine his frustration. He collapsed and they had to carry him away when he received the news that he had failed yet again. At last, he said he had been called upon by Jehovah to get rid of all the demons in China.

"You know Jehovah?" he asked.

"I heard Eva mentioning him," said Ning-ning.

Hong had gotten it into his head that he was the son of Jehovah. Ever hear of Jesus? He was Jehovah's son too, which made him Hong's brother! Hong formed secret societies, raised an army, and fought northwards to the Yangtze Valley. They called themselves "Heavenly Kingdom of Great Peace." Back then all the men used to wear their hair in braids. They cut them all off. They captured Nanking in 1853 and renamed it the "Heavenly Capital." They tried to reorganize the city, setting up schools and spreading their beliefs. So the Emperor had no choice but to stop Hong at any cost.

There were a lot of religious Westerners in China. Hong had met some of them and read their books. The Qing government had the support of the foreigners who weren't too fond of Hong and the way he claimed to be Jesus' brother and all. When their joint forces finally broke through the city walls and marched into Nanking, they burnt and killed for days and days, and turned the "Heavenly Capital" into hell.

171

"Worse than what's happening now?" Ning-ning asked.

Grandpa's Dad had told him it was very bad, but he had not seen it with his own eyes. Back then there were no tanks, planes dropping bombs, or machine guns.

The Jin residence was a good-sized compound with a main house and two wings enclosing a central courtyard. The family ran a teahouse as well as a well-known store in the Temple of the Confucius which specialized in selling rice paper, writing brushes, ink sticks, and other tools prized by scholars. It had all been burnt down. Several of Grandpa's uncles were killed trying to prevent imperial army soldiers from looting. Grandpa's own father suffered a broken rib. Great-grandpa, the patriarch of the clan then, couldn't take this strain and died even before the dust had settled and all the dead had been buried. Once Nanking had been retaken, the rest of the clan picked up whatever they could from the ruins and left. All except for Grandpa's father, who ended up staying in Nanking.

"Is that why we are still here today?" Ning-ning sounded really interested now.

"My father fell in love with a beautiful girl and decided to stay in Nanking after all."

"Where are the rest of the Jin family now?"

He knew they had wandered off to Fengyang in Anhui province. Some had stayed and took root there. Others had wandered further away and all contact was lost with them over time. He still remembered seeing his own grandpa once: an elderly man, gray-haired, moustache, soft-spoken...

"Just like you, Grandpa!"

"Yes."

Ning-ning giggled happily.

His grandpa, Grandpa continued, coughed a lot at night, too. Whenever this happened, his father or his mother would get up, pour him a cup of hot water, and pat him on the back until the old man was quiet again. His parents had wanted his grandpa to stay and live with them, but the old man wanted to go back to Fengyang. That was his new home now. He had three other sons and more than a dozen grandchildren there.

"So, if I visit Fengyang today," enthused Ning-ning, "I'll see lots of relatives there?"

"Yes, you will."

"Think of that! We should go and visit!"

"Maybe we should. Maybe it's time."

Grandpa's birth had caused so much pain to his young mother. It had been a very difficult birth. His mother had been in labor for two days and the pain was killing her. His father was waiting anxiously while his mother was moaning, delirious from the pain and the uncertainty. The frustrated midwife had told his father to go outside, go somewhere, but he remained. He wanted to hear the first cry of his child. and he wanted to know if his wife would be okay. He just sat outside by the door, waiting.

It was on the third night that he heard a baby's wail at last. It was a baby boy.

Years later, Grandpa was told that his mother had lost a great deal of blood and was not able to have more babies after that.

"My birth almost caused my mother to lose her own life. Isn't that a very bad wrongdoing on my part?"

"How could that be your fault?" Ning-ning said. "It took you three days to be born? You probably didn't want to come to this world because you knew there would be lots of suffering in it."

"That might be true," Grandpa chuckled, "but I don't remember thinking like that when I was being born."

"Oh, Grandpa!"

25.

"But, Grandpa," Ning-ning said, after a long pause, "I still don't know how you became a Buddhist."

"Remember how you used to ask me why you didn't have any uncles?"

"Yes?"

"Well, you should have had three uncles, all born before your mother."

"Really?"

"Your first uncle, if he were alive today, would be nine years older than your mother. He was born with a loud cry, ten times louder than the pitiable noise I had made when I was born."

Jin-ge, meaning Golden Song, was a very smart kid. He could read Chinese characters by age two and write by age three. His reading and hearty, musical laugh had brought so much joy to his young parents.

One evening little Jin-ge said he would go downstairs to play with Auntie Huang's big brother, Shi-tou, which means rock. It was a popular nickname for boys. Well, the two of them wandered outside and never came back.

"Auntie Huang's brother?" exclaimed Ning-ning.

"Yes."

"That means Da-mei and Er-mei should have had an uncle, too?"

"That's right."

The two families searched and searched for days, but they were gone. Just like that. Jin-ge's mother cried and cried. She waited day and night at the entrance to the alley and asked everyone she saw if she had seen the boy, but people only shook their heads.

Undeterred, she went on to say:

"He has this...here on his belly, a little purple birthmark, shaped like a bird."

"Like a bird?" Ning-ning asked.

"Yes."

"That's unusual."

"It is."

That birthmark was on Jin-ge's belly, always covered by clothes, and people wouldn't be able to see it. But there was no point explaining that to his mother. What else could she do?

"Is that the reason why you love birds?"

"Yes, I love birds that can sing."

"Like Larkie."

Grandpa nodded.

It was just the start of a very sad and tragic period in their lives. They had two more baby boys after that, but both died just days after being born. The folk doctors said there was something wrong with their mother's milk because she had been so sad. Some years later, a daughter was born, who survived.

"You mean Mama!" exclaimed Ning-ning.

"That's right. But only a year after your mother was born, your Grandma died. She had just been through so much. So much."

So one day he carried his baby daughter to the Soul Valley

Temple at Purple Mountain. Having put up two incense sticks and some offerings, he knelt down, and began to pray. But he didn't know exactly how. He just knocked his head against the hard floor as he had seen other people do.

"What are your wishes, young pilgrim?" A kind voice nearby asked.

He looked up and saw a middle-aged monk standing in front of him. Wisps of incense were curling upward. The monk's face was calm, kind, and serene.

He broke down and his sorrows poured forth in a torrent of unintelligible mumbling. He shook his head as the tears streaked down his cheeks. The monk remained calm, nodding his head as if he understood every sorrow.

"If you really want to be free from pain and suffering, young pilgrim," the monk said finally, "you should learn about Buddha. Only Buddhism can bring you enlightenment and put an end to suffering, which is one of the truths of all life."

"So it was then you—" Ning-ning said.

"Yes, I wanted to repent for all the wrongdoings and cleanse myself of all the evil influences. In the years since then it has given me so much peace and joy. That and when you were born!"

"Now listen," Grandpa continued. "I didn't know it at the time, but the man in the temple, that monk, he was a Japanese."

"What?" Ning-ning exclaimed.

The monk had come all the way from Japan because Nanking was home to so many famed Buddhist temples. I remember his name: Benevolent Truth.

"Did Mama give you much trouble when she was young?" Ning-ning asked.

"No, not at all."

Suo-zi, meaning "locked," so she would not be lost like her elder brothers, had given him so much joy. He loved her just as much as if she were a son, and taught her to read and write just the same. Never mind that she could not carry on the family name. She even went to school for a few years and grew up to be a fine young woman. For many years, Suo-zi had taken care of him like a perfect daughter. But as she grew older she caused him pain, too.

She wasn't a disobedient daughter. She was a loving, dutiful daughter in every way, but she had fallen in love with a soldier. It was the last thing he wanted for his daughter.

"Why is that?" Ning-ning asked, just as her mother must have done.

Because a soldier's life was to kill or be killed. That was all there was to it. The Jins had all been victims of soldiers.

"But this soldier is a different," Suo-zi had argued.

"How so?"

"He's a scholarly kind of soldier, a soldier who has brains, who has ideals."

"Such as?"

"Such as wiping out the warlords so people could live in peace and prosperity."

"But he'll have to kill for his ideals!" he had shouted furiously.

Yong-hui turned out to be not only handsome, but also intelligent, well read, and soft-spoken. He was like the son Grandpa could have had.

"Grandpa?" asked Ning-ning.

"Yes?"

"Have I given you any trouble?"

"All you have given me is joy."

"Really?"

"Yes. But remember when you grow up and—"

"Grandpa, I will never cause you any pain. Never. I Promise."

"I'm glad."

It was quiet now. Quiet for a long time. Grandpa could hear Ning-ning's slow, measured breathing. She was asleep.

He began to feel drowsy, but then began to chant silently, his lips moving without sound as his quivering hand moved the pearl-like strand in his hand methodically.

26.

When Eva stepped out from the bathroom and into the adjoining bedroom she stopped.

Stunned.

The bedroom, dimly lit by several large candles atop dressers, nightstands, and windowsills, was ghastly quiet. It was cold. The warm vapors all around her in the bathroom had been left behind.

In a large cushioned chair near a window a Japanese man was sitting cross-legged.

He was middle-aged and dressed in a short-sleeved robe. She caught sight of his eyes twinkling behind gold-rimmed glasses which reflected the flickering candlelight. He had a neatly groomed square of a moustache which moved slightly as his upper lip twitched.

The man must have been sitting there the whole time while she was bathing. Eva trembled with shame. The Japanese soldier had told her to leave the bathroom door open, but why didn't she shut it after he had left?

The man's eyes were on her. Feasting. In the dim light his eyes moved about hurriedly, watching her face, her throat, the shape of her body, all the way to her feet clad in delicate sandals with thick red straps. She could feel his eyes on her.

Without a word, the man rose silently, taking slow, measured steps toward her. His hands slowly clenched and unclenched.

Eva closed her eyes and stared at the floor. Oh, Father! Don't let that man touch me.

The man came right up to her. With his short, thick fingers he touched her chin gently and raised her head up. She saw him but could not look at him.

"No afraid, *guniang*," he offered awkwardly in Chinese. "I no hurt you, *guniang*."

He was about half a head taller than she. She could smell the liquor on his breath. His hand moved from her chin to her shoulder and slowly down her arm.

His hands fumbled at the sash around her waist. He straightened the knot, his hands lingering at her waist, then at her hips. He started to walk behind her. He laid his hands on her small, round shoulders and guided her slowly toward the bed. She closed her eyes.

Her shoulders heaved and the tears flowed from her eyes. She opened her eyes again. With hands still on her shoulders, the man had led her to the full mirror which stood on the floor next to the bed.

He pressed his head against the back of her head, his face and chin rubbing against her hair and neck greedily. His calloused hands clawed at her scalp, grasping handfuls of black hair. She could see his face in the mirror, and with his hands he held her head, forcing her to fix her gaze on the abhorrent ravishment.

The man's fingers went to untie the wide sash on the outer robe. Terrified, she raised her hands vainly but he pushed them down as she sobbed repeatedly, her shoulders heaving. She coughed and shivered uncontrollably. He pulled the sash away and let it fall to the floor. Slowly, his hands grasped the folds of

181

the robe and pulled them apart slowly. His eyes widened at the sight of her young, pale body. He moaned, and his hot breath was foul against her neck. He groped her now, touching her body underneath her robes. He pushed against her from behind and grasped her tightly with trembling fingers.

Oh, Father, come and save me!

He jerked the robes off her shoulders and they fell silently to the floor about her feet. She was completely naked now. She shivered. Her body was covered in gooseflesh. With terrifying strength he lifted her at the waist, carried her a few clumsy steps, and threw her onto the bed. Before she even had a chance to move, he fell on her.

She tried to fight but she had no strength; delirious now that she was crushed. He held her down, and forced himself machine-like upon her with a raging fury.

When she felt the pain it was as if she was being split in two, but only an empty blackness now swirled in her mind. Her body was somewhere else. It wasn't hers anymore. In her mind she searched for a ray of light in the all-enveloping darkness.

Save me Father!

But when the horror had passed she knew she was still alive. He had collapsed unexpectedly on top of her, moaning pitifully. A moment later he rolled away, drunk in his blind, lustful stupor.

Eva looked down at her naked body. It was red with bruises. Her thighs quivered uncontrollably, and when she tried to move the pain stung her again. The savage, monstrous thing was now heaving next to her.

She was cold now, and despite the pain she struggled to raise herself up. She looked around the room. It was the same as before. The candles burned faintly as the shadows flickered faintly.

As she sat up her head whirled. She closed her eyes again, then slid one leg slowly off the bed and onto the cold wooden floor. She struggled to stand, and the floor boards creaked underneath her as she took a few painful steps towards the crumpled robe as it lay on the floor in front of the mirror. As she crouched down to pick it up she saw her reflection: her disheveled hair, and the redness in her eyes and on her face. She turned away at once, clutched the robe with both hands, and held it tightly against her as she started to sob once more.

Then she heard a hideous cry coming from the bed. She saw the savage, monstrous thing come to life. It sprang from the bed naked, eyes staring blankly ahead as if it had glimpsed something horrific. It looked into the dim light of the room as if confused, disoriented, then ran about feverishly as if searching for something.

It had seen her, crouched on the floor beside the mirror, and it now flew into an uncontrollable rage. There was bright glint and a swishing, whispering sound in the air as it raised something high over its head. It shrieked at her:

"You toad! You filthy hag!"

She closed her eyes for the last time.

"Oh, Father. I come to you with this sullied body. Will you forgive my sins? Can I be one of your children, sit by your feet, and bask in your kindness and love?

A voice spoke, rushing toward her like a silent whisper:

"Yes."

Eva's lips froze in a wan smile as she hit the floor.

Thursday

December 16, 1937
The Fourth Day

27.

Ling awoke before the sun rose, the predawn wind cutting through his thin clothes and chilled him to the bone.

The skin of his face felt so dry and parched, as if at the slightest touch it would crumble apart. From the hot, burning sensation in his ears he knew that the chill blain he had developed was getting worse. It happened almost every winter since he had become a soldier. When spring came with its first gentle breeze, his ears would turn red and itch relentlessly. By mid-spring, when yellow-green shoots began to sprout from trees and the flowers began to bud, the old, dead skin would shed a tiny piece at a time to reveal a new layer of tender, soft skin underneath.

His hands were tied behind his back and had gone completely numb. He couldn't feel his fingers, nor even the wound on his heavily-bandaged hand.

His hands. He had used all kinds of weapons: rifles, pistols, machine-guns, even swords and knives, and wielded them with skill. But now, his hands were useless. They had once been capable hands, not just for fighting, but for many other things too: writing, painting, holding his wife, carrying his son on his back, and doing magic tricks to make his precious daughter shriek with laughter. But he had used them to kill. They were just about all used up.

It's one thing to kill your enemies in combat, he reasoned, but quite another to kill when your enemies have already thrown their hands up in the air. Even during the warlord era he had let go many an enemy combatant who had surrendered. Only once had he killed an enemy who had already been wounded: a poor lad who lay on the ground, his head resting against a shriveled tree trunk. He had a hole the size of a coin right through his throat. His face was white and nearly drained of blood. His eyes stared blankly ahead, and his wound bubbled as he tried to speak.

"Kill me," the lad had begged in a weak voice.

Calmly, Ling put a bullet into the lad's temple and released him from his pain.

The last thing he would tolerate would be soldiers preying on innocent civilians. It was a principle he adhered to way back when he was still a junior officer in the Nationalist Army. He had been so furious when he happened upon several of his soldiers looting away at Ginling College ten years ago during the Northern Expedition. He would have shot them instantly if they had not immediately dropped their spoils. He marched them back to the barracks and had them whipped in front of everyone. He had done the whipping.

And it was his hands that had gotten him into trouble with the Japanese.

It was yesterday afternoon when he was dozing at the University of Nanking Hospital when several dozen Japanese soldiers swaggered into the ward and ordered all the patients out of bed. They were looking for former Chinese soldiers, one bed at a time, one patient at a time. Soon it became clear that almost all young and middle-aged men in the ward would be suspected of having been soldiers before. They were hauled from the beds and taken away.

"I'm not a solider!" Ling had protested, once they had arrived at his bedside. "I'm a teacher!"

A young Japanese officer grabbed his unbandaged hand and squeezed it hard. Ling winced in pain. The young officer only smiled:

"Look hands! No teacher! Liar!"

He grabbed Ling by his collar and slapped him hard across the face.

Ling staggered. He could feel the Japanese officer's fingerprints cutting through his skin and burning permanent, shameful marks on his bones.

It was the first time Ling had been so close to the enemy he had fought so hard in the last few months. *If only I have a weapon in my hand! He thought. A pistol. A sword. Anything. The sword dangling at the officer's hip is so close, so tempting. No,* he decided. *Not here. Not now. It would be suicidal and it would hurt so many innocent people here.*

Ling got hold of himself.

Poor Little Chao-he looked the perfect age for a young soldier. The Japanese didn't even look at his hands but had just taken him away. The two of them had been tied up and were led out of the ward with the others.

Now, with the bone-chilling morning air slicing through his clothes, Ling rose to his feet and limped in a long procession of fellow prisoners. Without even looking back, he knew Little Chao was close behind him, trembling hard.

From the smoke and fire of China Gate to the mad, dizzy journey to the hospital, and now, ultimately, to this slow march to a certain, cold death. He did not think it would end like this. In the hospital he longed to see his wife, his son, his daughter, and his new son-in-law. He should have left with Little Chao and not have lingered for so long. One day earlier and he would not have been caught.

As he plodded along on this cold December morning, Ling felt wave after wave of throbbing pain pounding against his head. He looked about. There were men and women, all laboring ahead silently, head and eyes downcast. Behind him the procession reached back at least two hundred meters. There were five columns, and Japanese troops marched alongside, rifles pointed toward the ground, but there was no use in breaking free. In front of him to the right, an officer rode atop a magnificent horse. His sword dangled at his hip. The horse blew blasts of hot vapor into the crisp morning air.

Last night they had all been locked up in a cold, damp warehouse. The group taken from the hospital had joined a larger procession of prisoners this morning. The Japanese had rounded up everyone. It made no difference whether they were soldiers or not. Some of the women were taken away from the group and did not return. The children wailed and were left to wander the streets.

Now the pale morning light began to flood the sky behind Purple Mountain. The procession turned west, marching along streets littered with debris. As they marched on the small houses grew sparse and the land opened up. Ling knew they were headed toward West Water Gate.

He looked up and his heart sank. Ahead he could see that they were being led to a huge pit both deep and wide which had been dug in the ground. There were already many Japanese soldiers setting up machine guns along its perimeter. They drew closer and he saw the crumpled bodies which lay at the bottom of the pit, and the savage stench of death rose up to meet his nostrils. Ling held his breath. There were soldiers there. And many civilians. Their bodies had been shredded to pieces by bullets. Animals had come in the night and had strewn the entrails about. Bodies, and parts of bodies lay in heaps, crumpled and twisted, mouths agape, with empty eyes staring out from half-blown-apart heads, looking skyward for some salvation.

The men and women in the procession began to moan audibly and some dropped to their knees to retch violently before wailing in utter despair.

Ling's heart raced. He had no weapons. No chance. They were all going to die.

The columns had now lined up on all four sides of the pit. There were five rows of about forty people on each side. Ling could see Little Chao standing in front of him, a little to his left. He was looking at his shoes, but he was shaking violently.

"Okay?" Ling managed to whisper.

The young man gave a quick nod. His teeth chattered.

Poor Little Chao. There was nothing he could do to help him. He still remembered the first day they met nearly two months ago. They desperately needed new recruits to replace the heavy losses suffered from the aerial bombings. Little Chao had never shot a gun before. However, he was young, fast, and smart. Ling took to him at once.

It turned out that Little Chao was from the north. His family, like hundreds of thousands of other northerners, had joined the exodus of refugees after the incident at the Marco Polo Bridge outside Peking, where the Japanese army began to march to the rest of China.

They had fled quickly, always staying a day or two ahead of the advancing Japanese army. But the warplanes quickly over-ran them, and he had lost his little sister in Shanghai during a bombing raid. He made it with his parents to Nanking but they were killed soon after. In Nanking Little Chao had resolved to stand his ground defiantly. He would have made a great soldier.

Ling stood in silence. He winced as his head throbbed and his mind raced faster than he could comprehend. He had never looked back before, but now that certain death loomed in front of him with no hope of escape, the darkest recesses of his soul were suddenly laid bare.

He could see a kid huddled in a bag, blindfolded, gagged, both hands tied in the back, both of his little legs being bound, too. There was the sound of squeaking wooden wheels grinding slowly along a stone street.

How did the kid end up in the bag? Ling didn't know. It was night and the image faded to a blur, drowsily floating under the pale light of a hazy moon hanging low on the horizon.

But he could hear sounds. Gongs and horns, as if a parade were passing through the streets of Nanking, or a troupe of trav-eling entertainers, trailed by dozens of neighborhood kids.

Two kids emerge from the shadows, following the commo-tion of joyous noise and dancing, festive lights. Oblivious to their surroundings, they follow the procession in jubilation.

A rickety old wagon drawn by a sick looking donkey moves slowly along a narrow, pebbled street, its wheels grinding their way into darkness. One of the kids is on the cart. In the bag.

The kid wakes up later, but he find his parents at his bedside. A different smell is in the air. Incense sticks have been placed in a brazier on a nearby table, the thin wisps curling upward.

"Oh! You've come back!" cries his mother. Slowly she begins to feed him chicken broth. It tastes salty and delicious.

"Yes, eat well, and rest well," says his father.

A few days later, everything is fine. But somehow the kid knows that everything here is different. Everything.

"It's your fever," says his father. "It must have done something to your memory."

"We were so worried because you're such a special gift to us. A gift from *Guanyin* herself!"

"*Guanyin*!" he exclaims in wonder. The Goddess of Mercy.

His parents pull up his little jacket.

"Look here!" They tell him, pointing to his belly, "It's a gift from *Guanyin*!"

On his belly is a small purple birthmark. He remembers it well. Everyone says it looks like a bird.

"It is!" he laughs.

So there it was at last. Ling opened his eyes again. The pit of death yawned and bloated before him. He had never been convinced that he was a gift from *Guanyin*, and the happy memories from his childhood quickly faded with the passing of the years. His parents only smiled blankly at his persistent queries, but soon even those faded, but in his soul of souls he knew he was from some other place, abducted and sold to a family who had wanted a son to carry on their family line.

His eyes welled with tears and he blinked repeatedly. Ling filled his mind with happy thoughts, images of his soon-to-be-born grandchild. He would have no grave for them to visit, but for him, just to honor and show reverence to one's ancestors in some way was good enough.

The Japanese officer atop the horse barked orders, and the soldiers forced all the prisoners to turn around so that they faced away from the pit. They all fell to their knees, facing away from the pit.

A single Japanese solider was assigned to each column of five prisoners.

Nearing certain death, the wails grew to a crescendo. Others stood silently, waiting for the inevitable.

From the crowd nearby a commotion erupted. Ling turned his head.

A Japanese soldier was dragging a woman out from one of the prisoner columns. Her belly was fat, covered by a long, flowing skirt. She dropped to the ground, screaming hysterically. Other soldiers turned and guffawed. The officer on the horse seemed unconcerned.

The soldier dragged her to a mound of dirt next to the pit. He threw down his rifle and fell on top of her, his pelvis pounding away, utterly oblivious to the fact that he had just broken rank.

Beasts! Ling muttered to himself. Beasts!

But the woman fought fiercely. She bit and tore at the soldier's face, drawing blood. The other soldiers laughed hysterically at their naive comrade's predicament.

Enraged, the solider jumped up and spit at the woman, drawing still more laughs. He retrieved his rifle, and lunged with its bayoneted end at the woman's neck, but missed and stabbed instead the earth next to her head. She tried to raise her arms, but with lightning quickness the soldier withdrew the bayonet from the dirt and plunged it into the woman's chest, laying on it with all his weight, pushing it in deeply. She let out a bloodcurdling scream and tried to strike him one last time. She convulsed and writhed, nearly shaking the rifle out of his hands, but with all his strength he withdrew it, stumbling backwards. Blood poured forth from the wound and bubbled slowly out of the woman's mouth.

He cursed and spit at her again, and, coming forward, he cut open her belly from end to end. She let out a final bloodcurdling shriek as her intestines spilled out onto the dirt as the bayonet was thrust in repeatedly. Skewered, the quivering pink and grey fetus was pulled out at last into the morning light for a brief moment before being hurled away into the nearby dirt.

Ling closed his eyes.

"Little Chao," he whispered.

"Yes?" the young man replied, his teeth clattering.

"Stay close behind me," he instructed. "When I fall, fall in with me, understand?"

The young man groaned between convulsive sobs.

The officer on horseback gave an order and the soldiers unsheathed their swords. Along the ring of prisoners surrounding the pit, the head cutting began. Those furthest from the pit were killed first. Those kneeling next to them or behind them were awash with blood as each head was taken.

As the soldiers wielding the swords progressed down the lines, another group of soldiers would follow, at a safe distance, picking up the heads and arranging them neatly in rows. It was like some kind of ritual.

A soldier wielding the sword was coming to the prisoner right in front of Ling now. He paused for a moment to check his blade, then abruptly grabbed the hair of the man kneeling before him to straighten his neck, placed the blade on his shoulder, then sliced deeply, back and forth once, then twice. The man's tied hands clenched and unclenched furiously amid the spray of blood.

The warm, salty drops hit Ling in the face as the man's headless body fell forward.

The soldier now swaggered back for Ling.

This is the end, then.

Hui-ping. Helen. Dong-zi. And Peng-fei. I will see you again.

Ling felt a hand clutch his hair. He closed his eyes.

Something cold and sharp bit into the back of his neck. A second later it turned hot and sticky.

"Little Chao!"

He rushed into the air as if weightless.

Drifting downward, he was a withered leaf caught in an icy wind.

Darkness closed in.

28.

There had been no improvement with his breakfast.

The ham and fried eggs still tasted of fish, but Rabe didn't want to bring it up with Liang, his cook, again. A substitute cook was a substitute cook and until the war was over, he didn't have the time to go about finding a permanent, professional cook. Besides, Liang had probably, sincerely, tried his best. The way things were going, even Herr Kiessling wouldn't be able to come up with anything tastier. Even the bakery had been looted and there was nothing nice left to cook.

After breakfast, Rabe went directly to his car and started toward his front gate. As the gate was opened, throngs of women and children were kneeling on both sides of the driveway.

"Please let us in Mister!" they prostrated themselves before him.

"Please help us, Mister, we've no place to go!" Their voices were full of despair.

"We'll never forget your kindness!"

The young mother with a baby crying in her arms, the girl with messy hair and soot-blackened face, the elderly woman whose gray, cotton-padded clothes were already torn. They would be all be dead

Rabe exited the car and told the servant to hold the gate open.

"We've more than five hundred inside already, Sir," said the servant.

"We'll manage."

The servant opened the gate wide as the group of women and children helped each other to their feet and shuffled slowly toward the gate. As they approached Rabe they bowed deeply, almost afraid to touch him as if he were some kind of living deity, but mumbling gratefully as they passed into the compound.

With the gate closed behind him, Rabe headed toward Ninghai Road. When he reached headquarters, several of the Safety Zone and International Red Cross Nanking Branch members were already there. He got to work right away.

As had been expected, things had been getting worse. All the shelling and bombing they had experienced during the months before the Japanese entered the city were but a prelude to the horrors taking place now.

Thousands of disarmed former Chinese soldiers had been rounded up and butchered outside the Safety Zone.

At least fifty police officer he had hired to maintain order within the Safety Zone had been escorted out of the Zone and shot.

Countless numbers of women and young girls had been raped or murdered.

All shops outside the Safety Zone had been smashed open and looted.

Worse, reports of pillage, rape, murder, and disorder inside the Safety Zone were increasing.

Even houses displaying American, British or German flags had been broken into.

All houses occupied by German military advisors had

been looted.

There were so many problems to be taken care of, but so many were beyond his abilities. There was little he could do to stop the Japanese from rounding up former Chinese soldiers and murdering them in large numbers. He had to focus on the thousands of refugees inside the Safety Zone. No Chinese dared set foot in the streets now, let alone try to make it to a refugee center.

Rabe went over to his typewriter, put a clean sheet of paper in it, and decided to write a letter to Tokuyashu Fukuda, attaché to the Japanese Embassy, right away:

Mr. Tokuyashu Fukuda,
Attaché to the Japanese Embassy,
Nanking.

Dear Sir:

Yesterday the continued disorders committed by Japanese soldiers in the Safety Zone increased the state of panic among the refugees. Refugees in the large buildings are afraid to even to go to nearby soup kitchens to secure the cooked rice. Consequently, we are having to deliver rice to these compounds directly, thereby complicating our problem. We could not even get coolies out to load rice and coal to take to our soup kitchens and therefore this morning thousands of people had to go without their breakfast.

He paused.

Rabe knew he had to present, in unambiguous terms, the

severity of the situation without in any way offending the attaché and other officials at the Japanese Embassy. Simply put, he needed their understanding and cooperation to solve the problem. Besides, these embassy people hadn't shown themselves to be as barbaric as their military counterparts. From his dealings with them weeks ago about setting up the Safety Zone and his sporadic contacts with them in the last few days, he knew that the embassy staff had been unprepared for the brutality of the military operation. Rabe continued:

> Foreign members of the International Committee are this morning making desperate efforts to get trucks through Japanese patrols so these civilians can be fed. Yesterday foreign members of our Committee had several attempts made to take their personal cars away from them by Japanese soldiers (A list of cases of disorder is appended.)
>
> Until this state of panic is allayed, it is going to be impossible to get any normal activity started in the city, such as: telephone workers, electric plant workers, probably the water plant workers, shops of all kinds, or even street cleaning....

Just then Rabe's office assistant came in to tell him that Mr. Kikuchi, the interpreter for the Japanese embassy, was at the door.

"Please tell Mr. Kikuchi I'll be with him shortly."

"He has this note for you," the assistant said, handing Rabe a piece of paper:

> THE SO-CALLED 'SAFETY ZONE' SHALL BE SEARCHED FOR CHINESE SOLDIERS.

Rabe already knew that the army had commenced their mopping up campaign as soon as they entered the city. This piece of paper merely served as a courtesy note to legitimize their actions so they could conduct operations on a much larger scale.

Rabe took a deep breath and continued to type:

We refrained from protesting yesterday because we thought when the High Commander arrived order in the city would be restored, but last night was even worse than the night before, so we decided these matters should be called to the attention of the Imperial Japanese Army, which we are sure does not approve of such actions by its soldiers.

Most respectfully yours,

JOHN RABE	LEWIS S.C. SYMTHE
Chairman	Secretary

Rabe then walked into the reception room, where Mr. Kikuchi stood up to shake hands warmly. The interpreter was wearing a dark wool overcoat. The smile on his face was genuine and he was every bit as modest, polite, and charming as any other young man Rabe had ever met.

"Mr. Rabe," the young interpreter said, "the note that I've just delivered is from the Imperial Army."

"I understand."

"What I am really here for," Kikuchi hesitated for a second, "is to have your cooperation to get electricity and water running again as soon as possible."

"That, Mr. Kikuchi, depends on two things," Rabe said. "One, the machineries at the electricity plants having not being destroyed by bombing and shelling; two," he coughed to clear his throat, "the safety of the Chinese workers must be guaranteed. Given the incredible behavior of the Japanese soldiers during the past few days, I'm afraid not too many Chinese workers will be very eager to go and fix things and get the machines running again."

"There is no denying," Kikuchi said in a lower voice, his face flushing with noticeable embarrassment, "that the behavior of some of our troops has not been the most exemplary in the last few days, but in the interests of—"

"I'll see what I can do if the Japanese army will guarantee the safety of Chinese workers."

In a few minutes, they were already on Sun Yat-sen Boulevard North, on their way to Lower Pass Dock where the main power plant was located.

They sat in the car silently. Their eyes probing the now empty streets. Neither said anything for a long time.

"Mr. Kikuchi," Rabe broke the silence, finally. "When do you think all this mess will be cleared away?"

"I don't really know," the young man said, "but I hope soon. Right now the Imperial Army is otherwise occupied and—" he stuttered.

"I know, but I also hope that they will at least let others do it. You know the Chinese Red Swastika Society associated with our Committee?"

"Yes, I've heard of it. A charity organization."

"Well, they want to mobilize all of its members and go out

to bury the dead, but they have been forbidden to do so. That's something I just don't understand. The dead deserve the decency of a burial. When the dead are properly taken care of, the city would return to some sort of normalcy again. Wouldn't that reflect well on the Japanese army?"

"I agree. However, Mr. Rabe, I can't help wondering some-times—"

"Go ahead."

"Forgive me. But why are you, a German, taking such risks on behalf of the Chinese?"

"Nanking is also my home.

"I beg your pardon," the interpreter said, blushing.

The power plant had been abandoned for over a week now. Carts, wheelbarrows, willow baskets, and shovels for conveying coal and cinder were scattered about. Luckily, though, except for the roofs missing shingles and the walls being marked by clusters of bullet holes, the buildings and the chimneys still stood intact. Inside, the generators, controls, electrical transformers, gauges, and other equipment looked intact too.

"It could be running again within days," Rabe said, "but we'll need at least one engineer and forty to fifty workers to make things happen. That's the problem."

Given the behavior of the Japanese, finding workers to run the plant would be next to impossible. The chances of finding a competent engineer would be very slim, too. He could probably call on one of the German engineers in Shanghai, but not until things quieted down in Nanking. Right now it wasn't safe for anyone, Germans included.

"I'll report back to the Consul General and see what we can do about it," Kikuchi said.

Later that afternoon, Reverend Magee came knocking on the door. He carried his portable motion picture projector.

"I just got this developed. It's what I've filmed so far."

Rabe and Magee drew the curtains as Magee mounted the reel. The projector began to roll in Rabe's darkened office. Magee narrated the scenes:

"This was an eleven-year-old girl, standing with her parents near a dug-out in the refugee zone as the Japanese enter the city; the soldiers kill her father with a bayonet, her mother with a rifle-shot, and give the girl a horrible slash in the elbow with a bayonet."

"This is the corpse of a boy, about seven years old, who died three days after admission into Dr. Wilson's hospital. He had five bayonet wounds in the abdomen, one of them perforating the stomach."

"Here's the corpse of a man who has been taken from the Agriculture Hall of the University of Nanking, with about seventy others, who were all bayoneted or sprayed first with rifle fire, then with gasoline, and set afire."

"Here's a clerk in an enamelware shop who was bayoneted in the head simply because he could not produce any cigarettes when a Japanese soldier demanded them. The wound was so severe it cracked open the skull and you could see the brain."

"Here are two Buddhist nuns who were raped by a gang of Japanese soldiers; the little one, apparently an apprentice, only eight or nine years old, was bayoneted several times in the back after the rape; the sixtyish nun was shot in both legs; both nuns were left in the temple to die."

"The horror an eight-year-old girl has been put through: A

gang of thirty some Japanese soldiers come to the Ha house in the southwestern part of the city, and demand entrance. When Mr. Ha, the landlord, a Mohammedan, opens the door, they kill him immediately with a revolver shot. Then, they shoot Mr. Xia, the eight-year-old's father, whose family is in hiding in the Ha's house, and who has knelt before the Japanese begging them not to kill anyone else."

"Crying over her husband's still warm body, Mrs. Ha asks the Japanese why they have killed her husband. A soldier puts a bullet into her head. Mrs. Xia, the girl's mother, is dragged out from under a table in the guest hall where she has tried to hide with her one-year-old baby. After being stripped and raped by the soldiers right on the spot, she is bayoneted in the chest, and then has a bottle thrust in her vagina, the baby was sliced in two with a bayonet."

"Several of the soldiers then go to the next room where the eight-year-old girl's grandparents, aged 76 and 74, and her two elder sisters, aged 16 and 14, are hiding. They drag the girls from under the bed and are about to strip them when the grandmother tries to intervene; she is killed with a revolver shot, as is the grandfather with his dead wife's body in his arms."

"The two girls are each raped by two or three soldiers repeatedly. Afterwards, the younger girl is bayoneted to death while the older girl is stabbed and subjected to the same horrible treatment as her mother, this time, using a sharp cane."

"Then, the Japanese soldiers go after the remaining people in the room: the eight-year-old girl, and Ha's two small children, aged five and two respectively. The five-year-old is bayoneted to death while the two-year-old is cut in half from the neck down."

"Miraculously, the eight-year-old survives with a bayonet wound. She crawls to the next room where lie the bodies of her mother, her father, and Mr. and Mrs. Ha with their small baby. She finds that her four-year-old little sister has escaped the fate of being slaughtered. The two sisters live on puffed rice and rice crusts for days until they are rescued by their neighbors."

Rabe stood up abruptly, looking at the grainy images in silence.

"I've got to get a copy to the *fuehrer* as soon as I can. He might have second thoughts about Japan."

"I wouldn't count on it," Magee replied.

29.

Grandpa had been moaning since late last night.

He had been shaken by fits of coughing, leaving him gasping for air, his chest heaving.

"Grandpa, are you all right?" Ning-ning asked, patting his back gently.

"Yes." Grandpa's reply was weak, unconvincing, accompanied by another fit of coughing and wheezing.

For Ning-ning, it had been quite exciting to learn that Grandpa had lots of relatives in Fengyang. Maybe they could help, but they were so far away. She had never been to Fengyang, though she had gone with Mama to Hefei and even Qingtao to visit Papa.

She didn't want to lose Grandpa. He had always been in her life. His daily chanting in his soft, humming voice had been one of her earliest memories.

"Grandpa," she said softly. "Tell me what's wrong." It was the tenth time she had asked. Every time Grandpa had just shaken his head and kept moaning.

"The food," Grandpa mumbled at last. "And the water." He wheezed and gasped again.

She hadn't thought about it but Grandpa was right. The cold steamed buns were very old, dry, and powdery. And it was difficult for Grandpa to drink cold, unboiled water. He always had a small bowl of hot soup at the end of his meal: a few slices of bean curd, green beans or spinach leaves, and a finely chopped green onion on top. It seemed like such a luxury now.

Ning-ning had another idea.

"Grandpa," she said. "I'm going to make you hot tea."

He looked at her, puzzled.

"It will help you. I'm sure it will."

"Don't," Grandpa shook his head. "It's too risky to start a fire."

But she was already tiptoeing toward the main room.

Late afternoon was drawing to a close. The sun was sinking slowly in the West. Looking out the window, Ning-ning could see the swaying branches of the prune tree outside, and the row of buildings that were still standing along the Sun Yat-sen Boulevard North. But beyond that, a haze lingered in the air. The city was engulfed in thick dust and smoke.

Ning-ning was in the kitchen now. She could see several items which had been thrown on to the floor. Their small stove was overturned and lying on its side, cinders and coals were scattered about the floor. There were a few broken bowls, cracked cups, smashed plates, and their old, dented, metal water kettle with its wooden handle. There were small glass jars and wooden boxes. In the fading light it would be difficult to find what she needed.

She crouched to the floor and searched with her fingers, feeling about, careful not to touch broken glass or anything with a sharp edge.

She found a box of matches, crushed by a heavy, booted foot. Nearby she found the box containing the tea as well. When it had fallen most of the tea had spilled onto the floor, but she gathered up what she could. She also found the wood chips used to start the stove. The vat they used for water had a big crack now. Luckily, there was still enough water left near the bottom.

Ning-ning searched for Grandpa's favorite teapot, only to discover the small shards of maroon clay lying smashed on the floor. The teapot was old. Grandpa had been using it for as long as she could remember. It was made from a special clay from Yixing county, and whenever tea was brewed in it, it held the flavor of the tea, so that over time, the teapot itself developed its own wondrous fragrance. Ning-ning held one of the pieces to her nose and smelled it. She found the small lid nearby, which had rolled away but did not break. On the top was a small carving of a smiling Buddha. She placed the lid back on the shelf.

She had to make do with other vessels now, but she couldn't find any unbroken bowls or cups. What about the smoke? If she lit a fire it might be seen from outside.

She walked to her bedroom and examined a cotton quilt which had been thrown off the bed to the floor. Gathering the soft folds, she took it back to the kitchen, and, balancing herself carefully on a chair, she punched the fabric through two nails sticking out of the wall above the kitchen window. The quilt hung, covering the window, and sagging a little bit in the middle. Now, no one from outside could see in.

Slowly, she went to the front room and opened the front door carefully. The hallway was quiet. A few feet away, the stairs led down into darkness.

Satisfied, Ning-ning returned to the kitchen, and proceeded to set the small stove upright again. She put in a few wood chips and some scraps of paper that she found. She attempted to strike a match, but it sputtered and died out; feeble wisp of smoke curled upward. She tried again. Still nothing.

With the third match she succeeded in getting it lit. The flame erupted in blue and then settled down to a warm, glowing yellow. She reached into the stove and set the match underneath the wood chips and the crumpled paper.

The paper caught right away. She placed a few longer pieces of wood on top, and soon they glowed at the edges. Smoke started to pour from the stove. She threw in a few more small chips of wood and more paper.

She blew on the fire gently. The yellow flame licked the metal grate on the top of the stove. The wood crackled and one or two small embers floated upward. She put some water in the kettle and placed it on the stove.

"What are you doing?" asked Grandpa.

"Making tea. But, your teapot. It's..."

"Broken."

"Yes. But the lid is still good." She said, coming back to his bedside.

"Never mind. There is another teapot somewhere in that trunk. There in the corner."

The old wooden trunk was not large but it was filled with all kinds of small memorabilia and family keepsakes. Ning-ning had seen them all before, though she never noticed a teapot. She remembered the short bamboo flute with brown and black patterns and golden tassels; a hand-knit scarf and a pair of pillow cases with two birds embroidered on it; and a few small bundles of yellowed rice paper with calligraphic writings. There were also a few pairs of fluffy, red padded baby shoes, and a toy drum.

"See it?"

"No," she said, still feeling around in the trunk. "You mean this?"

"That's it."

It was a bundle wrapped in deep red cloth. She took it out and carried it to Grandpa's bed. Grandpa untied the silk ribbon at the top. Inside was a small wooden box. He opened it in front of Ning-ning.

It was only a bit larger than a grownup's fist. It was an exquisite teapot in the shape of a bird. The bird's beak was the spout. The clay was deep red and its surface was smooth. On the side of the pot some Chinese characters had been carved.

"This is a Bird Sutra pot," Grandpa murmured, "Your Mama gave it to me a long time ago."

"You want to use it now?" It seemed so special.

"Why not?"

Ning-ning returned to the kitchen with the new pot. The fire continued to burn. She put a few more small pieces of wood on the fire.

She then put two spoonfuls of Rain Flower tea leaves into the pot. Taking the kettle from the stove, she poured in some hot water—just enough to rinse the leaves, as she had seen Grandpa do countless times. She put the lid on and poured the water out. She added water again, this time being careful not to have the water come up too close to the rim of the tea pot. She put the lid back on. With a kitchen towel as cushion to help support the hot pot, Ning-ning carried it toward Grandpa's room, gingerly, minding every step, so that the tea would not spill. She set the pot down on the small nightstand.

Grandpa looked at the pot and closed his eyes.

"It's wonderful!" he exclaimed, drawing the fragrance deep into his lungs.

Ning-ning smiled.

30.

Rabe was about to return home that afternoon, when Mr. Katsuo Okazaki, the Consul General of Japan, came to call.

"All the refugees must leave the Safety Zone and return to their homes." He said this with care and concern in his voice. He was sitting on a sofa across from Rabe, holding a cup and saucer of coffee in one hand. Behind him several members of his staff stood at attention silently against the wall.

"May I inquire as to why, your Excellency?" Rabe asked.

"Because we want them to go home and open their shops as soon as possible so that life will return to normal again."

"As to that, sir," Rabe said, "I am in agreement with you. However, I believe you have seen enough with your own eyes to know that it is not safe for anyone to return home yet. Last night alone, at least a thousand women and girls were raped."

The Consul General looked up from his coffee. There was a moment of awkward silence. Then he put the coffee down on the small table in front of him. He cleared his throat.

"We understand there have been isolated instances of less than exemplary behavior on the part of some undisciplined soldiers," the Consul General offered. "But, such behavior should be expected from any army upon entering a city as large as Nanking. Do you see my point? You know of the fall of Constantinople, the Spanish Conquests, and, of course, the liberation of Peking from the Boxers?

"Yes," Rabe interrupted, "Japan was part of that alliance."

"Mr. Rabe, history has not endowed the British, the Americans, or the Germans with any moral superiority to lecture Japan. She knows exactly how to treat the people of a country she has just conquered after incurring heavy loss of life."

Rabe fumed silently.

"As a matter of fact," Okazaki stood up, his face twitched as he spoke. "The Imperial Army of Japan is here to liberate China from Western imperialism which has been like a scourge on its history for a hundred years. The civilizations of Asia shall now prosper together...."

Nanking would serve as an excellent example of such prosperity! Rabe wanted to interject, but held his tongue.

Rabe stood up too. "Yes, it is a grand plan, your Excellence," Rabe said, as they turned toward the front door, "But the reality we are facing now is that it is simply not safe for any refugees to return home. I'm also very concerned about those soldiers who have surrendered and have been disarmed."

"Your concern is greatly appreciated," Okazaki said. They were at the front door now. "We know that some Chinese soldiers have been shot," Okazaki lowered his voice. "But we did not anticipate there would be so many prisoners taken. I have received word that a detention camp will be set up on an island in the Yangtze. From this time on, all prisoners shall be treated as humanely as possible."

Rabe escorted Okazaki to his car. The Consul General bowed politely before he and his entourage left. Rabe sighed deeply.

It was dark outside when Rabe got in his car to go home.

He drove along Ninghai Road, past the entrance of Ginling College. Clusters of soldiers were loitering at the front gate in complete darkness. Rabe slowed but did not stop. No one was safe anymore. If the Japanese viewed him as uncooperative, what chance did he have? They could carry on without his help. Rabe shook his head and sighed.

A servant opened the gate of his compound and he drove inside. There were women and children huddled together on the grass, under trees, along garden paths. The car's headlights were switched off and the compound was plunged once more into darkness.

There was very little food and water. What would happen to them if he were gone?

He was their only hope now. The Safety Zone had failed. The walls to his compound were the last chance for these people.

He looked back at the front gate again. There were several dark shapes moving in the shadows outside, and a shuffling sound made by booted feet. Retrieving his flashlight from the car, he strode to the front gate. Flicking the light on, he saw several Japanese soldiers peering in the gate. They laughed hoarsely, stepping back into the shadows. He could smell the smoke from their cigarettes.

Rabe went right up the gate.

"*Deutsch*!" he shouted, enraged. "*Heil Hitler*!"

31.

They sat together in near darkness as Ning-ning lifted the lid off the teapot.

A fragrant aroma greeted her nostrils. The tea was ready. She lifted the pot, placing the towel underneath it, and presented it to Grandpa. Grandpa's hands shook as he took it.

"It's hot."

Grandpa took sips slowly and noisily directly from the pot.

"It's good." He said. "Just hot enough."

Grandpa took another sip, like a kid that hadn't been fed for days.

He sipped again. A few drops dribbled down his chin.

"Should I add more hot water?"

"Not yet. Don't want to be too greedy. Greed will only lead to misery."

"Are you feeling any better?"

"It's so warm."

Grandpa breathed deeply. The hot, fragrant tea was working, Ning-ning thought. If only she could done this sooner, but lighting the fire would have been too risky.

"You would make a good nurse," Grandpa said. The teapot quivered in his hand, but he held it steady, and took another sip.

"Aren't I a good nurse already?"

"Yes! Yes! You're the best nurse."

"I want to be a teacher," said Ning-ning.

"Teaching," Grandpa repeated the word slowly, savoring its meaning. "The Jins, you know, have always been teachers of sort. Not exactly like the schoolteachers today. More like private tutors."

"You told me before."

"Did I?"

"And you said it was the noblest of professions."

"It's true."

"And...Confucius was a teacher, and so was Mencius. And who else?"

"Chuang Tzu," said Grandpa.

"That's right. He was a sage."

Grandpa paused for a few moments, then spoke, "It's enough water for me. Let's take care of the stove."

Guided by the glowing light of the stove, Ning-ning felt her way to the kitchen, opened the stove's vent door and looked inside. Flames no longer rose up to lick the kettle. Only a few embers still glowed warmly. She closed the door and tiptoed slowly back to the darkened bedroom. She felt her way to the coffin and climbed inside. As her eyes adjusted to the darkness, she could see Grandpa's form reclining in bed, the beads moving through his quivering fingers.

Slowly, she drifted off to sleep.

Friday

December 17, 1937
The Fifth Day

32.

As soon as she finished lunch, Minnie Vautrin went to the front gate again, just as she had done in the morning each day for the past several days. There, she saw more streams of weary, wide-eyed women, girls, and small children. They kept pouring in. She guessed there were at least 9,000 in the campus now. Something had to be done.

Fortunately, the University of Nanking, which was also within the Safety Zone, had opened up a few more of its dormitories. Some of the women and children would be taken there, and she would lead them through the streets. The University of Nanking campus was not too far away, but with so many Japanese troops everywhere, it would be very risky. Already groups of refugees were being lined up in the quad. They huddled together. The college staff kept telling them they were going to the University of Nanking, where shelter could be found.

Minnie had reached the front gate and looked out into the street, close behind her was a long column of women and children.

Gangs of Japanese soldiers were going from house to house in the area right outside the campus. They swore, kicked down doors, smashed windows, and carried away whatever they could. Others merely loitered across the street or stood aimlessly in front of the gate.

She turned to address the women and children right behind her,

"Everyone! Hold hands!"

Everyone joined hands as they proceeded slowly out of the college and into the street. The women and children were shaking with fear but Minnie stood in front, leading the long train, always looking in every direction.

Right away a group of soldiers rushed up to them, stopping just a few feet away to admire the sight. They looked for young woman and girls, made faces, and cried out:

"*Huaguniang*! Ha Ha!"

A bold Japanese soldier swaggered up to a young girl walking just a few feet behind Minnie, grabbed her arm suddenly, and tried to pull her away.

The girl was terrified, but she held the hands of the woman in front of her and the one behind her. They continued to walk as the soldier held her arm.

Minnie rushed to the girl's side.

"Let her go!" she demanded.

The solider stared back. The procession had come to a halt. Other Japanese soldiers laughed but kept their distance.

The soldier gave Minnie a hard look, waved his rifle in the air, and let go of the girl's arm.

Minnie's body trembled, but she maintained her intense gaze as the soldier walked away. The repercussions for a Japanese soldier shooting a Westerner would be severe, so she had assumed, but what guarantee was there that any of them were really safe? She turned back to the front of the line and made a huge waving gesture with her arm. They started off again. A half hour later they were at the University of Nanking campus. Fortunately, the Japanese troops had not molested them any further. Relieved, Minnie sighed as the last of this group of refugees filed into the campus.

She told Helen and a few other staff members who had been assisting her to return to Ginling College first, then made the rounds to insure and comfort as many women and children as she could. On her way back to Ginling, her pace was quick but she did not show any outward signs of fear. The soldiers watched her silently but did not trouble her.

A short time later, Minnie reached the Ginling gate, but something was different. She stared at the front of the school for a long time before it hit her.

"The flag! The flag is gone!"

The huge 30-foot Stars and Stripes was gone.

A custodian shuffled alongside Minnie and told her that while she was away, two Japanese soldiers had lowered the flag and cut it from the flag pole. He pointed to the steps in front of the science hall where it lay on the ground in a heap.

"They are searching the dormitories," the custodian said.

Minnie hurried to Central Hall with the custodian. Two soldiers there were pulling and kicking at its main door.

"What's going on?" Minnie spoke firmly but maintained her composure.

"Open the door please!" one of the soldiers, short, stout, with a small moustache, growled.

"I don't have the key."

"Soldiers here!" growled the other solider.

"No soldiers." She shook her right hand for emphasis.

The soldier with the moustache leaned toward her and slapped her hard across the face. She saw a brief flash of light, and her glasses fell halfway off her face. She put her hand to her cheek. It stung as if on fire.

Never in her entire life had anyone hit her like that. Minnie trembled with shock and anger.

"Open the door!" the soldier repeated.

"Side door," Minnie said to them, pointing. "Try the side door."

The two Japanese soldiers entered through the side door, rifles drawn. They searched, room by room, every floor.

A short time later they came out. Minnie saw three workers being led through the door, their hands tied behind their backs.

"What's this!" Minnie demanded.

"Chinese soldiers!" snarled the Japanese soldier with the small moustache.

"No! Not soldiers! Workers! Gardeners!"

But the Japanese soldiers ignored her. They took the three Chinese men toward the front gate.

When Minnie reached the front gate, she saw a large group of Chinese men kneeling beside the road. Mr. Li, Mr. Xia, and a number of workers, groundskeepers, and other college staff. A Japanese officer was in the process of interrogating them.

"Who's in charge here?" the officer demanded, turning to face her.

"I am," Minnie stepped forward.

The officer came up to her and growled, pointing to the men: "Which one servant, which one soldier? Speak!"

Minnie identified Mr. Li, Mr. Xia, and most of the others as the college staff. She tried to explain that they had taken on extra help and she did not know everyone by name.

Just then she heard a car rumbling to a stop right outside the gate.

George Fitch, Lewis Smythe, and Reverent W. P. Mills, all of the Safety Zone Committee, stepped out of the car.

Minnie clasped her hands together.

The men were met with bayonets and were escorted inside the gate.

"Stand in a line!" the young officer barked at them nervously. "Remove your hats!"

There was nothing inside their hats.

The officer ordered all three to raise their arms so that a soldier could search each of them for weapons.

"The International Safety Zone Committee has been approved by the Japanese Embassy," Fitch said to the officer loudly.

The officer remained unimpressed. There was a dull blankness in his eyes. Perhaps he hadn't understood a single word Fitch had said.

"*Parlez-vous français?*" Fitch volunteered. It was worth a try.

"*Oui,*" replied the officer, to Minnie's surprise.

"*Formidable!*"

Fitch's French was slow, but fluent. Minnie picked up a word here and there, but couldn't really follow the conversation. The Japanese officer was struggling to follow everything Fitch was saying too, but at least they were talking. After a few moments, the officer left to talk with a group of soldiers who listened in rapt attention. He soon returned and addressed Minnie and the men:

"All foreigners leave!"

"Leave where?" Minnie asked.

"Here," the officer glared at her.

"But this is my home. I can't leave."

"All foreign men leave!"

The three were duly escorted back to the car. It was useless to resist. Minnie knew that the help she had counted on was gone. Ginling College was on its own.

The car had no sooner rumbled away than a piercing scream came from one of the nearby buildings.

A Japanese soldier darted to the front gate. He bowed quickly and spoke to the officer, who nodded and gave an order to a group of soldiers. A moment later they had all departed in the direction of the side gate.

It had gotten very quiet. Minnie and all the others remained where they were, some standing, some still kneeling by the gate. They were not sure if the Japanese soldiers had really left, or if they were even allowed to move.

After several minutes of silence, the gateman shuffled slowly outside the front gate and looked out into the street.

"They've gone!" he whispered to the others.

They all got to their feet, unsure of what to do next.

Big Wang, the groundskeeper, came running toward them out of breath.

"They've left by the side gate! They've taken two girls from East Court," he reported, heaving, "and at least twelve girls from the Science Hall!"

Minnie hung her head in silence. They had been fooled.

33.

Helen was exhausted.

She had helped to escort over 4,000 women and girls to the University of Nanking campus. It was a long, slow-moving procession, and each step felt like an eternity. Her legs were sore, but because they had all joined hands and marched together, they had been allowed to make the procession unmolested and she was thankful for that.

When she returned to the campus with Blanche and a few other members of the college staff, the first sign of trouble they encountered was the American flag lying crumpled at the entrance to the Science Hall. As they drew closer they could hear shouting and things being thrown about inside the hall.

There were at least thirty Japanese soldiers searching the building room by room, herding all the women and children into the central hallway.

"Who's your commanding officer?" Helen had demanded, unafraid. She had learned a lot from watching Minnie.

A soldier with a sword at his hip looked Helen over up and down contemptuously.

"Who are you?" the officer demanded in his heavily-accented Chinese.

"I'm a teacher here," Helen replied. She could feel her heart pounding in her chest. "What's going on?"

"Chinese soldiers hiding here!" the officer said.

"This college is a refugee center. There are no soldiers!"

"Soldiers hiding!" the officer growled.

"Where? Where can they hide?" Helen gestured wildly with her arms.

"In rooms," the officer said, "And in *here*!" The officer pulled at Helen's skirt, laughing, and then turned away.

The soldiers resumed their search, throwing desks, chairs, books, all over the floor. There was nothing Helen or anyone else could do to stop them. She stood there in the hall watching, frightened, and furious.

The soldiers had gone down the entire length of the hall. Now they were coming back to where the officer stood. The soldiers talked animatedly for several moments, then proceeded noisily toward the central hallway and the front door.

Women and girls were huddled against the wall. Suddenly, the soldiers reached out to grab as many young women as they could. The girls kicked and screamed as they were herded out of the building. There were terrifying cries of "*Jiuming! Jiuming!*"

Save me! Save me!

Helen yelled out as loud as she could, "*Zhushou*! Stop!" But they ignored her.

She followed them out of the building. She caught up with two soldiers who were carrying a girl no more than fourteen years old between them.

"Let go of her!" She screamed.

"Another *huaguniang*!" one of the soldiers called out hoarsely. "Take her!"

Two other soldiers came up from behind Helen, grabbed her arms roughly, and began to pull her along.

"Let go! Let go of me!" Helen protested. She was terrified.

"Ha!" said one of the soldiers, poking her face with his thick fingers, "A real *huaguniang*!"

Yet another soldier came up and, grabbing her legs, they picked her up and carried her right out of the campus.

Blanche came running out, hysterical, but there was nothing she could do.

"Stop it! Stop it!" she screamed, "She's going to have a baby!"

34.

Sun Yat-sen Gate towered in front of Brigadier General Nakamoto.

It was at least twenty meters high. Its broad, puffed out chest of gray limestone fanned out on both sides, stretching out as if bathing in the glorious sunlight. The gate had such an awe-inspiring presence, Nakamoto thought, yet it was no match for the warplanes, bombs, and heavy artillery. The soldiers of the Japanese Imperial Army had swarmed into Nanking and the city was theirs for the taking. The spirit of the Hongwu Emperor must have been disturbed by the sound of the victorious Japanese warriors pounding the very ground these walls were supposed to protect.

Nakamoto was with a group of brigadier commanders. He could see General Matsui Iwane, commander of the Central China Expeditionary Force, and Prince Asaka through the backs of more than a dozen divisional commanders and top staff officers—General Yoshizumi Ryosuke, General Suematsu Shigeharu, and so on, all atop tall, strong-limbed steeds.

They had been part of the victory procession marching through the grand, arched gate. As they entered the city, a thunderous cry arose:

Banzai!

Banzai!

Banzai!

Thousands upon thousands of Japanese soldiers were arrayed alongside Sun Yat-sen Boulevard East. Their bayonets shimmered fiercely against the ever rising sunlight.

Nakamoto saw General Matsui Iwane raise his right hand to his temple smartly in salute. Camera shutters clicked as flash bulbs went off in unison. Nakamoto caught glimpses of Imai Yoshio of *Asahi Shimbun* in the crowd of newspaper correspondents busy taking snapshots and scribbling notes to describe the scene.

Prince Asaka was the new commander of the Shanghai Expeditionary Force, and had been very pleased when he heard the reports from Nakamoto and the other units three days ago. General Matsui, however, seemed more concerned with how the international community would react to the mopping-up campaigns once the word of what had happened in Nanking reached the rest of the world. Matsui wanted to hold a memorial service for the war dead tomorrow-all war dead. Nakamoto was glad that all of the divisional commanders and top staff officers had voiced their objection to the idea, in chorus, when General Matsui proposed it at a meeting before the ceremony. Asaka didn't utter a word in support of General Matsui. The prince stood there, staring ahead, his eyes blank, as if he were not at the meeting at all. In the end, minding the sentiments of almost everybody else present, General Matsui changed his mind.

Matsui was experienced but old and frail. He no longer grasped what was at stake here, Nakamoto felt. Hold a memorial for the cowardly Chinese? He could not bear to think of the idea. Now that Prince Asaka was in charge, the Imperial Army had what it took to take all of China if it wanted. Asaka was sharp-minded and resolute. Wasn't that the reason the Emperor had sent Asaka to replace Matsui only days before the liberation of Nanking took place? Changing top commanders at a critical moment like this was no different from changing horses in the middle of a swift river.

The victory ceremony was so grand, filling Nakamoto's heart with so much pride. The soldiers sang and cried out joyously, their voices echoed in the air.

Now that it was over, Nakamoto, accompanied by Zenba and a dozen of his soldiers, proceeded to return to his headquaters.

Suddenly, a dark, grey cloud drifted overhead and blocked out the sun.

The world dimmed.

A fierce wind suddenly picked up, whipping the dust which swirled among the horses and soldiers lining the streets.

A sign? An inauspicious sign?

But the men carried on.

Nakamoto was annoyed with himself. He had allowed his mind to consider superstitious misgivings just as he had allowed those hysterical young girls to haunt him in his sleep. Their twisted, twitching bodies, severed limbs, and the torn *shiromuku* soaked with blood.

But he had not done anything that was not in the name of the Rising Sun and all its glory.

He breathed more easily.

Already a ray of sun had found its way through the dark cloud.

He looked at the sky again. Perhaps there would be snow. That would be good. The air was not clean here. In his mind he could see the snow. He was back upstairs, looking out the window. The world outside was covered in a layer of pure white, silky snow.

And after a long, hot bath, he could sit in his chair by the window, sipping warm *ginjo-shu* sake and watch the snow fall in Nanking, the capital of China.

The city had not disappointed him. At least, not as far as its *huaguniang* were concerned.

The young girl he had the day before yesterday was so pure and chaste. She would have been perfect, truly perfect, if only she had not tried to cover herself with the kimono afterwards. His *shiromuku*! How could she have done that? Why did she want to cover her body? He had already taken her. He was her *mizuage* patron. What was there to cover, anyway?

But she was gone, and Nanking looked like a ghost town again.

The streets were empty. They had used the Chinese to clear away most of the debris along the main thoroughfares at least. After that, the rest of the mopping-up campaigns proved to be extremely effective.

Should he send Zenba in search of another girl again? He would have his way. He felt more like a hunter than a commanding general. What's the difference, anyway? He grinned.

35.

When the victory procession led by General Matsui Iwane and Prince Asaka emerged from Sun Yat-sen Gate, the sky shook with deafening cries of joy by the columns of soldiers standing at attention along Sun Yat-sen Boulevard East.

So glorious was the sight, the line of soldiers thrust forward and stretched seemingly without end right into the heart of the city itself.

Imai Yoshio, the special correspondent from *Asahi Shimbun*, raised his camera again to catch this historical moment, undoubtedly a turning point in Japan's military campaigns in China. He had followed the march into Peking, then the push into Shanghai, and finally the taking of Nanking. This triumphant moment was without question the highlight of his coverage of the war so far, and his eyes grew moist. But something had been gnawing at the back of his mind all day.

Imai had a clear view of General Matsui Iwane in the lens now. The general's slight yet upright body poised atop the grand steed, his feverish face, the glitter in his eyes.

He depressed the shutter.

As he steadied himself, the camera in his hand whirred and clicked. The thing that had been disturbing him suddenly ballooned forth: dead Chinese—men, women, and children—piled in clearings or open spaces, falling where they had been shot, sprawled along at the base of bullet-ridden city walls, and heaped along the banks of the Yangtze River.

He remembered them now. The piles were still smoking when he came upon them, white teeth and pink flesh visible beneath the charred, blackened skin doused with kerosene and set aflame. Bodies swept into the Yangtze, pink and bloated, bobbing incessantly, whirling day and night under the quay.

He filed past the trembling, vacant stares of old people, women, and children as they saw their sons, husbands, fathers, and brothers—several hundred of them—all huddling together in open space near the *Asahi Shimbun* branch office, being dragged forth six or seven at a time to a half—crumbling brick wall blackened by fire. Each was shot with a single bullet to the back of the head or a savage bayonet thrust to the back of the neck. It took hours.

At dawn, he hears the sound of footsteps shuffling along the icy street. Dashing out of his room in the *Asahi* office, he sees a seemingly endless procession of Chinese, tied together with ropes and wires, being led by Japanese soldiers.

"Where are they going?" he asks, curiously.

"To the Lower Pass Dock, outside Water Front Gate," a junior officer throws him a reply.

Imai follows. He wants to find out what will happen to these people; most of them look like civilians.

The shivering cold of the December morning cuts through his wool overcoat. The ends of his fluffy scarf flap about him. In the early morning darkness he turns to look at the people strung together, straining to read their faces. But there is nothing in their eyes. Slowly, he allows himself to fall back, and after a while the procession passes him, leaving him behind.

Imai is about to turn back when the sound of machine guns roaring to life makes him jump up violently and cover his ears. Then he stumbles and falls to the ground. The guns are drumming all around him. The shots are coming from somewhere nearby. He gets up off the freezing ground and runs forward amid the cacophony to find another junior officer.

"What's happening?" he asks, shouting.

"We're killing them off. Can't you hear?" replies the officer.

"Killing them off?" Imai echoes blankly.

"It's the only way. There's too many of them!"

There is suddenly silence but the shots pound on and on in his head. The guns roar to life again. Another volley. And another.

Imai follows on the heels of the officer. The river is not far ahead. The sound of water splashing can now be heard. Imai has his hands over his ears, anticipating the next volley, but the shooting has stopped.

They are at the Lower Pass Dock now. Past another couple of buildings and they will be able to see the river.

Imai stops in the still-grey morning light, unsure of what his eyes are seeing.

The dock is completely buried beneath thousands of twisted, mangled bodies.

They rise up from the river, piling up all around the dock. Two large machine guns are placed up high, overlooking the riverbank.

There are several dozen human shapes wandering amid the bodies, grasping lifeless arms and legs, and hurling them tumbling end over end into the river below.

Slowly, the sun begins to rise.

Imai can see that the human shapes disposing of the bodies are not soldiers but Chinese coolies. At last, they too are made to line up along the riverbank, clothes bathed in blood.

The machine guns roar to life again.

The coolies tumble backward, their heads blown apart and their chests explode in crimson spray as they fall into the water.

A minute later it is all over.

Imai was panting furiously. He rubbed his forehead and blinked again and again as if to empty his mind of the horrific vision.

The sky turned dark and ominous. General Iwane and Prince Asaka had passed by already. He had to get to work. Everyone at home would be waiting anxiously for his report. He began to see it come together in his mind:

Nanking, special correspondent Imai, December 17: On this day of shouting and excitement, the cheers of one hundred million countrymen resound. Today, the deafening cries of banzai rising to the top of the city wall are the marvel of the century. Jubilation is breaking out here, in a bold, splendid ceremony to celebrate our entrance into the city. It has been four months since this army assembled its troops for the march into the heart of China, and as the magnificent result of our fighting, we have captured the enemy capital and gained ascendancy in all of China. Here, we have established the foundation of peace in East Asia. Can anyone look at the Rising Sun flag waving so magnificently over the headquarters of the Nationalist government without tears of emotion?

As he tries to convey to his homeland the actuality of the extremely majestic and soul-stirring grand ceremony, the pen of this reporter trembles with excitement. Over Nanking are clear skies like those of Japan, deep blue and clear and not a single cloud ....

36.

"What are the next two lines?" Ning-ning asked, her eyes fixed on the ceiling, trying hard to remember.

"I scratch my head, and my gray hair has grown
   too thin,
It seems, to bear the weight of the jade clasp
   and pin."

It was Grandpa's voice murmuring from his bed. Grandpa had a way of reading ancient poems with an almost musical cadence.

"Grandpa, how could Tu Fu know how we feel today?"

"How we feel today? He wrote that poem over a thousand years ago, remember?"

"Yes, but he speaks of wild times, our country crumbling, the weeds growing in the Capital, three months of fire burning in the skies, and—" she paused.

"And what?"

"—family letters worth ten thousand gold in price."

"And what else?" Grandpa persisted.

"And...gray hair getting too thin."

"That's me, not you!" Grandpa chuckled.

Grandpa paused to catch his breath,

"Winter will be over soon, then spring will be here. You'll see flowers bloom, hear birds twitter. It will be a time of joy, not sadness."

"Besides," continued Grandpa, "Tu Fu was talking about Chang'an, the old capital of the Tang Dynasty. Now, Li Po, he wrote a special poem about Nanking."

"Really? What is it?"

"Well, it goes like this." Grandpa coughed to clear his throat, and began:

> On Phoenix Terrace once phoenixes came to sing
> The birds are gone but still roll on the river's waves
> The ruined palace's buried 'neath the weeds in spring
> The ancient sages in caps and gowns all lie in graves
> The three-peak'd mountain is half lost in azure sky
> The two-fork'd stream by Egret Isle is kept apart
> As floating clouds can veil the bright sun from the eye
> Imperial Court now out of sight saddens my heart

"Why is there so much sadness in this poem also?" she asked.

"Because, it's like I said, there's so much sadness in life, I guess."

"So, the Imperial Court in this poem," Grandpa said, "is in Chang'an again."

"Because Li Po lived around the same time as Tu Fu?"

"That's right. Li Po was about ten years older than Tu Fu. However, the Phoenix Terrace, the ruined palace, and three-peaked mountain, and just about everything else—"

"—are here in Nanking?"

"Right."

"But I've never seen the Phoenix Terrace. Where is it?"

"It was in the southwestern part of the city, not too far from Worry-You Not Lake. But it had disappeared even before I was born. Destroyed by time and war I guess."

Grandpa sighed, then coughed again. Ning-ning could hear him wheezing faintly.

"Are you all right, Grandpa?"

"Mmmm."

Yesterday's hot tea had made Grandpa feel better. Ning-ning resolved to make more hot tea today. With any luck it would take care of Grandpa's cough and stomachache for good.

Ning-ning stretched out as she lay in the coffin, then slowly climbed out.

"Where are you going?" Grandpa asked.

"I want to make tea again."

"It's too much trouble."

"One more time," she insisted. Perhaps after tomorrow the Japanese would all be gone, and making tea, let alone hiding, would no longer worry them.

It had been an unusually quiet day. No gunshots. No explosions. There was an occasional noise of a door being closed or a voice calling out something vague and unintelligible, but by and large their world was quiet.

In the early afternoon, the sun suddenly disappeared. The sky grew overcast with dark clouds and the wind whipped up the dust in the streets.

She was in the kitchen. She reached for her quilt which was still hanging over the window when all of a sudden she stopped. In the distance, faint, but unmistakable, she heard a chorus of shouting rise up and float through the sky. Grandpa heard it too, and he sat up in bed, straining to recognize any sound, any word. And then they both heard it.

It was the sound of singing.

37.

Helen awoke on the earthen floor in a large, dimly-lit room.

She was hit again by a spasm of pain in her belly. Her fore-head was bathed in sweat. The rough manhandling she had suf-fered must have hurt the budding life inside her, too.

Pale light crept in through boarded up windows. There were other women and girls sitting alongside her. Her head rang with the words from her alma mater's song:

> And as we strive abundant life to give
> Abundant Life—your motto is our goal
> We pray that we may ever worthy live
> Of you—your dream of service in our soul

It was the motto of Ginling College. Helen remembered singing the song with tears of joy and pride during commence-ment in June. Now....

"Miss Ling," a young voice murmured next to her. It was the girl she had tried to save earlier. The girl was sitting next to her, dabbing her forehead gently with a handkerchief. She must have been in one of the study groups or games Helen had organized. "What's going to happen to us?"

"Are we all going to die?" another woman asked.

"I want you to know something, sisters," Helen murmured,

"No matter what happens, just remember that God loves you. God loves us all."

She was not a fully converted Christian yet. She still had too much Chinese in her veins to embrace the foreign religion whole-heartedly. She felt that she could find the same message of loving and serving one's fellow human beings in her native Chinese culture.

Still, the mere uttering of "God loves us all" at this moment in her life had made her feel better, stronger, less scared. In her eyes, whether the God she invoked was Jesus, Heaven, or any other supreme, divine being, was not really relevant.

"If God loves us all," the woman said, "Why doesn't He come and save us?"

"I...," Helen was caught off guard. "God knows what's going on here," she recovered. "He will come and save us all. Eventually. I know that for—"

The women looked sullen and miserable, sitting in silence. No matter what Helen said she could not assuage their fears.

The silence was suddenly shattered as the door was thrown open and at least half a dozen Japanese soldiers swarmed into the room. They started to grab the women and girls sitting closest to the door. The women kicked and screamed hysterically but were picked up and led away.

Oh, dear God, Helen prayed, whoever You are and wherever You are, please come and help us!

Another group of soldiers then followed the first, and rushed in to collect the rest of the women still in the room. Sobbing, shrieking and guffawing filled the room again.

Helen saw an officer walk in to the room. He was short and thin. His eyes fell on the women and he examined them greedily.

His gaze moved to Helen.

The young girl, who had been sitting next to Helen, was picked up by a soldier.

"She, sick, very, very sick." She managed to stutter before being led away.

But the officer did not take his eyes off of Helen.

Only the two of them were in the room now.

Helen could hear hysterical screaming drifting into the room. The sounds were coming from all around: upstairs, down the hall, the next room.

The officer began to circle around her, like a hungry dog, slowly, cautiously, his eyes fixed on her all the while.

Like a crouched lioness Helen bolted upward at the moment she thought he had least expected. She grimaced with pain as she tried to stand. She grabbed and tugged the officer's legs and pounded her head into his abdomen. She reached for the officer's sword and tried to unsheathe it.

She knocked him to the floor. But as he tumbled he pulled her with him.

She could feel that the officer panicked. Even as they rolled on the floor, she could see the glitter of shock and fear in his pupils.

He was short, small, and thin, but he quickly seized her wrist that still tugged at the sword and smacked it hard against the floor. Helen screamed out in pain but did not release her grip.

With her other hand she scratched at his neck digging her fingernails into his chin.

The officer threw wild blows, sometimes missing, sometimes striking Helen in the face or on the shoulders. But she did not relent. If she could just get the sword.

They thrashed and grappled on the floor. She bit and kicked and cussed furiously.

She was surprised by the amount of foul language she actually knew but had never used it. It just kept pouring out of her mouth as she fought.

The two continued to grapple and roll on the floor. Neither was able to gain the upper hand.

Failing to fend off the totally unexpected attack, the officer screamed something in Japanese. He screamed again and again, like a swine that had been tied up to be slaughtered.

A moment later she heard the shuffling of heavy boots, the door burst open amid shouts of laughter. But the laughter died even before the echoes of the footfalls had faded. She could hear the urgency in the voices of the soldiers who had just entered the room:

"Hai! Tajima-sama!"

She caught sight of them drawing their bayonets and lunging toward her, but she and the officer kept grappling, kicking, and rolling on the ground, making it difficult for them to aim and stab her.

Suddenly she felt a sharp, burning sensation in her right leg as she straddled Tajima.

They've stabbed me, she thought vaguely.

She felt another slash, another, another, and many more, in her legs, in her arms, in her face... her flesh was cracking up all over her body.

She could feel warm blood gushing down her face, blurring her vision, filling her mouth. It tasted salty.

Her hands loosened their grips.

Her breath became shorter, harder, shallower.

Oh, baby, she heard a voice murmuring sadly inside her, I'm so sorry. Mama can't protect you now....

And she let go.

The moment she crashed on her back, dizzy, she caught the cold glint of steel rise up slowly, then come plunging down onto her belly.

Everything went black for her.

38.

Nakamoto and his procession were entering a city square not very far from his headquarters.

He knew that turning left at the square would lead him to Ninghai Road. Near the entrance of this road was the big compound which housed the Safety Zone Committee. Following Ninghai Road for ten to fifteen minutes, he would be right at the front gate of Ginling College for Women. He could picture it all clearly in his mind, as if he had been there.

As he marched on, reliving again and again the victory procession which was still so fresh in his mind, a vibrant ray of sunlight cut a swath through the grey sky, bathing Nakamoto and his men in sudden radiance.

The troops behind him let out a loud, exhilarating cheer.

A few soldiers broke out singing. Others joined in fervently:

> You and I are cherry blossoms
>   of the same year,
> Even if we're far apart
>   when our petals fall,
> We'll bloom again in the treetops
>   of the Capital's Yasukuni Shrine.

At the first note of the song, Nakamoto shivered. He had

visited the Shrine on top of Kudan Hill in Tokyo. What an honor it would be to have died for the Emperor and to be enshrined there. Okaa-san would be so proud of her son.

They marched on through the square. Nakamoto's eyes scanned the buildings. They looked as miserable as ever, pitiable houses with collapsed roofs and crumbling walls. His eyes fell upon an opening in the street, a small lane emerging between two shattered, crumbling buildings.

Peering down the alley, Nakamoto could see that it zigzagged between a mass of hoary old houses with drab grey walls and blue-grey tiled roofs. But in the midst of this gloomy scene deep in the alley a single, magnificent prune tree stood in front of a small, old two-story building. It was truly a marvelous sight in this burned, bombed out section of the city.

Nakamoto steadied himself on his horse and raised his binoculars. Now he could see clearly that on the tree's upturned branches were clusters of delicate, purple buds which turned reddish toward their very tips.

Nakamoto's heart pounded. Right behind the tree, in the lower corner of an upstairs window. It was unmistakable.

A young face.

Despite the soot and the messy tresses in her hair, the face looked pure and beautiful. The eyes, large, liquid, were gazing intently in his direction.

Nokamoto breathed lustily. She would be the *huaguniang* for tonight.

39.

When Ning-ning pushed the quilt aside to open the window, she felt a sudden draft of cold wind in her face.

The sound of singing grew louder. Even the rice paper bandage in the window buzzed.

"What are you doing?" Grandpa half-shouted from the bedroom.

"Just want to see who's singing," she whispered back.

"Who else could it be?" Grandpa sounded irritated.

"Just a glance, Grandpa, I'll be careful."

A man riding on a horse came into view in the distance. He didn't pass quickly by, but stopped, looking down the alley. The sound of singing was all around them now. She saw a few other people cluster around the man on the horse. They were wearing uniforms. They looked like Chinese, but...

Just then she heard heavy footsteps and men's voices coming into the yard.

Ning-ning leapt away from the window as if scalded. Why hadn't she heard them coming?

She crouched down by the floor as the cold wind blew the quilt about wildly. Her heart pounded. Not daring to breathe, she stumbled and crawled along the floor back to Grandpa's room as quickly as she could.

She could hear boots shuffling downstairs and pounding up

the squeaky staircase now.

"Hurry!" Grandpa whispered hoarsely.

"What about you?" She climbed and fell flat into the coffin.

"Don't move, no matter what!"

"Sorry, Grand—" She shut the lid above herself.

"Shhhh."

They were inside their home. The Japanese were already inside their home.

They were inside Grandpa's room now.

She could feel it, like she had felt it the last time they were in here.

They stopped howling, but she could feel their ominous, frightening presence.

The air inside the coffin quivered, but she didn't hear Grandpa reply. Is he playing sick, or dead again?

Then she heard things being kicked at, thrown, tossed around, someone using something sharp, metallic to knock around under Grandpa's bed....

Someone coming closer to the coffin, so close that she could feel him right at her feet, so close that he could probably see through the lid and see her huddling inside the coffin.

She stopped breathing altogether, but her heart thumped loudly.

With a loud, animal-like scream, something sharp, metallic had been thrust through the lid.

Though it was dark inside and she couldn't see, she could feel its deadly presence. When it was pulled back, a faint light shone through the narrow, thumb-sized hole in the lid. It was right above the little space between her feet. What if she had been lying with her head at the other end?

But there was no time for her to think now. The next instant she heard a horrible, heart-piecing cry:

"Noooooooooooooooooooooooo!"

She knew that voice.

Something soft and heavy fell to the floor.

"Graaaaaaaaaaaaaaaaaaaaaaandpa!"

She screamed as she pushed open the lid and bolted upright in the coffin.

Ning-ning breathed hard. Her face was flushed. In the room, surrounding the coffin, stood three Japanese soldiers. They stared at her blackened face in astonishment.

The upper half of Grandpa's body, face down on the floor, was sprawled close to the edge of his bed. His right hand was stretched out as if reaching for the coffin. The beads lay loosely between his fingers.

On his back was something dark and wet. A Japanese soldier stood over him, a bloody bayonet in hand.

She screamed again, trying to step out of the coffin and run to Grandpa.

"*Huaguniang*!" All the Japanese soldiers shouted at the same time.

The soldier standing next to the coffin, a sword in hand, grabbed her collar and dragged her out of the coffin.

"Grandpa!" She wailed, and collapsed at his side. "You've killed him! You've killed him!" she screamed. They looked like us, Grandpa had once told her, and she had been curious. But now all she had was burning hate. They've killed Grandpa! They've killed Auntie Huang and Uncle Huang and Da-mei and Er-mei and so many others! They're going to kill me! They're going to kill me, too!

A hand gripped her shoulder. She jerked her body free, grabbed the soldier's hand with her own hands—small as they were—and bit into it as hard as she could.

The Japanese gave shrill cry. He pulled back his hand and struck her across the face again and again. Ning-ning crumpled to the floor as her head exploded with pain. The soldier fell on top of her, pinning her arms behind her head with a bone crushing grip. Her wrists went numb. She felt the full weight of the soldier on her tiny body. Rough, hideous fingers groped her, tearing at her clothes.

"*Jiuming!*" Ning-ning shrieked with every last breath as she kicked and thrashed her legs about.

She was hit hard across the face again and she tasted the blood in her mouth.

She went limp.

40.

When Brigadier General Nakamoto entered the upstairs room, with Zenba at his side, he was met with another wave of loud, lustful laughter.

A group of goddamn bustards had got in one step ahead of him.

The laughter stopped.

At one end of the room, where everything had been turned upside down, stood two soldiers. Their smiles died on their faces when they saw the general come through the door.

"Kuroda!" one of the soldiers shouted. "Come out now!"

"Wait your turn Ueno!" came the reply.

"Get the hell out of here now!" barked Zenba, the general's orderly.

The two soldiers moved towards the door. Zenba slapped each man hard in the face and gave each two kicks in the ass before letting them go.

Then, Nakamoto saw Kuroda stagger out of the bedroom, still fumbling with his belt buckle. The soldier mumbled in protest. The next instant, he glimpsed the General and froze, his eyes nearly bursting with terror.

Nakamoto was dizzy with anger. The insolent bastard! Wasn't' this the newly-commissioned officer who didn't even know how to dispose of those prisoners that one day?

Nakamoto's grip on the handle of his Sadamitsu tightened.

"Get the hell out of here," Zenba barked again, "Or I'll skin you myself!"

Shaking uncontrollably, Kuroda dragged himself a step or two forward, then froze again.

Nakamoto had already drawn his sword. With lightning speed he raised it into the air, and struck.

Kuroda's head tumbled from his body as blood shot forth, spraying up onto the ceiling. The warm, salty drops fell all about the room, and on Nakamoto's face and glasses.

Nakamoto stepped over the fallen body and walked to the room where Kuroda had just emerged.

An old man was sprawled on the floor. Blood trickled out from a hole in his back. Something large and dark lay against the wall. A coffin.

And on the floor next to the old man was the *huaguniang*.

Her eyes were closed and her face was bruised and swollen. She had been half stripped: her pants were pulled down to her shins. Bruises covered her white legs and belly. And as for her thighs....

She had been defiled!

She was not the *huaguniang* he had seen any more. Tonight, he wouldn't be able to sit by the window, watch the snow falling, sip warmed sake, and listen to the tinkling sound from the bathroom.

Seething with rage, the general raised the blood-bathed sword again.

He let it fall.

Something descended upon him suddenly.

Something tiny, primal, unearthly.

A blur of feathered, whirling fury

Whatever it was, it caused his sword to miss its mark, and he checked himself as it fell upon him. The whirling blur launched a fierce assault upon his face and head, trilling shrilly all the while. He shielded his eyes for almost at once he felt its fierce razor-like pricks on his head, his nose, and his cheeks. It struck again and again, moving and fluttering at lightning speed.

It was Nakamoto's turn to be terrified now.

It had all gone horribly wrong. The prune tree had beckoned him, only to make him glimpse the open coffin and suffer an attack by some winged devil.

Would he still be enshrined atop Kudan Hill in Tokyo? What would he come back as in the next life? It didn't matter. Nothing mattered. As long as it was not a filthy, disgusting toad.

"*Okaa-san!*" the general screamed suddenly, and ran out of the room, right past Zenba, and out the door.

Once he was atop the mare that had been tied to the plum tree in the yard, Nakamoto spurred it urgently and galloped away, never looking back down that alley.

41.

When Ning-ning felt her head hit the floor, she tried to open her eyes.

She squinted, but there was only darkness. She felt herself floating, like a bird soaring into the sky.

The air is cold up there and the wind blows through her hair. She can feel the presence of many people—her friends, neighbors, classmates, people she knows and doesn't know?—all going somewhere. Where are they all going?

In front of her is a figure, floating on the wind. The figure of an old man in a long gray robe.

"Grandpa?" she calls out.

But there is no answer.

"Grandpa!" she calls out again at the top of her voice, but no sound seems to have come out of her mouth. "It's Ning-ning!"

The old man turns his head.

"Why," the old man murmurs in a familiar, soft voice, which sends off a faint, melodious echo in the sky. "It's Ning-ning. Why are you here?"

"I want to go with you!" she replies, a rush of joy and sadness in her heart.

"Go where?"

"To wherever you are going!"

"I'm going to look for your mama."

"Me too. And look for Papa too!"

"No." Grandpa's voice is gentle but firm. "Go back. It's a long, long journey."

"You're angry with me!" She cries, "That's why you don't want to take me with you!"

"No. I'm not angry with you. But, you're not ready."

"When will I be ready, Grandpa?"

"In a hundred years, maybe." Grandpa chuckles.

"That's too long!"

"We'll all be waiting for you."

"Who are *we*?"

"You'll find out. We'll be waiting for you. I promise."

The wind has picked up and Grandpa's words, being tossed around more fiercely, becomes less clear.

"Be strong and...remember: You won't be alone in your world."

The wind has picked up and it's harder to hear Grandpa's words. He is going further and further away now. He is gaining speed, leaving her further behind. She sees him disappear at last into the mist.

She begins to drift back, airily, like a snowflake falling to the ground.

Ning-ning opened her eyes.

She could feel her finger move.

She wiggled her toe.

She began to move her arms and legs, but the pain suddenly tore through her again, and she felt its icy grip in every limb. She looked down at her naked body, covered with bruises.

Beasts! Monsters! What had they done to her?

"Grandpa?" she stammered. She saw Grandpa lying on the floor, the back of his head covered with messy, silver hair.

"Grandpa?" she whispered, "Did you find Mama?"

No answer.

Grandpa was dead.

No, he was not dead. She had just seen him. He was going somewhere where there would be no misery, no suffering, and where he could find Mama and many others who were dear to him.

She struggled to sit up, putting her pants back on, not looking at her bruised legs.

Grandpa's hands were still warm. She put her arms around his shoulders and tried to lift him, but she could not. She tried to turn him over, slowly.

When she saw his face the tears came pouring down her cheeks.

If only I hadn't wanted to see.

If only!

With one hand holding Grandpa's head, she reached for a pillow and rested his head gently on it. On his bed, under the pillow, had been placed the lock of her hair the day that she had cut it. Ning-ning took the hair and put it in Grandpa's still warm hand, closing his fingers around it. Taking a silk handkerchief from her mother's drawer, she gently laid it across Grandpa's face.

Suddenly, she heard a faint rustling, fluttering sound next to the coffin.

It was Larkie. He was on the floor. His wings twitched feebly and his tiny body jerked. Around him several feathers lay scattered. His black eyes still shone in the fading light of dusk.

His cage lay on the floor on its side, half smashed; the little door dangled open, hanging from one unbroken hinge.

"Kiddo?"

She picked Larkie up, brought him close to her face, felt his soft feathers against her skin. Larkie's wings twitched a few times as Ning-ning set him down next to Grandpa.

She found two incense sticks and a cold, steamed bun. She placed them on the nightstand and lit incense sticks with a match from the kitchen. She fell to her knees and prayed. Prayed for Grandpa, prayed for Mama and Papa, and prayed for everyone she had ever known. Her lips kept moving though nothing coherent came out. Tears gushed out of her eyes again and streaked down her swollen cheeks.

Outside, the snow was falling.

She had to get out.

Ning-ning felt her way slowly, cautiously, almost tripping over the body lying in a pool of blood by the front door. She didn't stop to look. She didn't want to see. She was in the hallway now, at the top of the stairs. She started down the steps slowly. She was by Auntie Huang's door now.

She stepped outside into the cold, wet air of the alley.

She felt the snow on her face. Slowly she felt it start to melt away her dry, salty tears and ink-stained face.

More snow fell, covering her hair, the ground, the twigs and branches of the prune tree so only the purple and pink buds shown through the whiteness. The whole world was drowsing amid the growing dusk, shrouded in a glistening, downy veil.

The fresh snow crunched crisply under her light footfalls. She looked at her footprints which wound their way along the alley back to her house. Soon they would all be covered, she thought.

She looked behind her again. Everything was quiet.

She trudged on, shivering. She had left the alley behind. Her face, her hands, her feet, her whole body felt so cold. Through the drifting snow she could see the opening of Ninghai Road not too far ahead. Suddenly she stumbled and fell face first into the snow. Her cheeks stung and she tasted the cold snow. She took a handful of snow and rubbed it all over her face. And another. And another.

Looking ahead, she saw only pure, misty white snow falling in the distance. With clenched teeth, she struggled to get to her feet, took a few steps, staggered, and fell again.

This time, she felt herself falling down slowly, dreamily, like a drifting snowflake.

Saturday

December 18, 1937
The Sixth Day

42.

Two hundred and ninety-eight.
Two hundred and ninety-nine.
Three hundred.

Ning-ning counts as she struggles up the steep granite steps. They don't seem as steep as when she was small, though. Back then, she had to hold tight to Papa and Mama's hands and kick her little legs as high as possible to make it to the next step. She chuckles at the thought of those days.

Just a few more steps and she will see them, the "Three Principles of the People" carved on the tablet above the entrance of Dr. Sun Yat-sen's memorial hall. She stops. As usual, Grandpa is way behind, at least fifty steps below. But she can hear him gasping hard.

"C'mon, Grandpa!" she calls out, trying to catch her own breath. "The way you're going, we'll never be able to get to the top." She giggles. Her giggle sends a loud echo across the vast, misty valley of green pines and cypress trees rippling all around and below.

Grandpa looks up, smiles, waves, and continues to climb.

A few small clouds drift lazily, brushing the tip of the sun-bathed Purple Mountain. Even under the vast, bluish sky, the mountain has a towering, majestic presence, overlooking the city drowsing down there with a serene, maternal indulgence.

Somewhere down there to her left is the Soul Valley Temple and to her right the Mausoleum of the Hongwu Emperor. She wanted to visit those places, too, to run through those gigantic stone statues of otherworldly animals guarding Hongwu's long gateway again, but Grandpa said another day.

"I'll wait for you up there." She waves to Grandpa and continues up.

She is inside the memorial hall now, tired, breathless, but in very good spirits. The echoes of her footsteps reverberate all around.

Papa and Mama are here too!

How?

She runs and throws herself headlong into her mother's arms.

Papa smiles broadly.

Grandpa has finally caught up.

They are all inside the burial chamber, looking into a circular pit excavated out of the ground. Sun's coffin is not black or made of wood. It is carved from exquisite white marble and on top is the carved marble figure of Sun himself, sleeping, lying in peace.

"It's so grand," Papa marvels.

"Yes," sighs Grandpa, "but all is empty when one dies."

"You won't die, Grandpa," she says. "Never, right?"

"Right!" Mama affirms.

They are at the rear of the memorial hall now. She sees a little trail there. Shaded by tall pines, cypresses, and other trees, the trail is flat for some twenty meters; then, it becomes very steep, winding upward, and disappears from sight.

Where will the trail lead to? She wonders. It has to be the peak of the mountain. It has nowhere else to go but up to the peak. And the view from there must be incredible.

"Where are you going?" Papa calls out as she races along the trail.

"I just want to see!"

"But Grandpa is already tired," Mama says.

"I'll help Grandpa." She hurries back, gives Grandpa her hand. Now, the four of them are walking on the trail together.

A short while later they come to the top of Purple Mountain.

The wind is much breezier up there, the sunshine more radiant. The city of Nanking, the hometown of the Jins for so many generations, is nestled down there in the sun-bathed mist.

"Can you see our home?" she asks.

"Can you?" Grandpa teases, still holding her hand.

"Yes, it's over there." She points at a westerly direction. "It's a small, old house with a plum tree covered with blossoms."

"And," Grandpa chuckles, "I think I see a little girl there too, looking out the window."

They all laugh.

Just then, a mournful, anguished cry rushes through the air from tree to tree. The birds scatter and take flight.

The ground underneath her starts to shake, as if the mountain were being seized by a monstrous demon, as if rows of long, venomous swords were unsheathed and reveling in some devilish dance, before rending and slashing everything in its path to shreds.

Terrified, she turns to grab Papa and Mama's hands. But they are not by her side any longer.

"Papa!" she screams. "Mama!"

They are nowhere to be seen.

Grandpa is gone too.

She flees down the long, winding trail, stumbling, tumbling head over heels, screaming in terror at the top of her lungs. Down, down she continues.

The mountain rumbles and surges. Something the color of blood pours from its summit and cascades downward, smothering everything in its path and turning the mountainside to smoldering ashes.

She stumbles down the long, steep granite steps. The blazing liquid crashes down right behind her. She can feel its heat splashing against her neck. The granite sizzles and cracks. The air is poisoned and birds fall dead from the sky at her feet.

She trips and rolls headlong down the stairs.

"*Jiuming*! Grandpa!"

"Don't be afraid, my child, I'm with you." It's a kind voice. A voice from somewhere safe.

Grandpa is at the bottom of the stairs. How did he get there?

Grandpa doesn't seem to be scared. His creased face stares at the furious mountain, and he chants in his soft, melodious voice. Grandpa opens his arms. She is running blindly toward him, but she trips and falls right past his outstretched arms, sliding and skidding helplessly away.

Snow. All around her is snow.

"Papa! Mama! Grandpa!" She screams again.

"Don't be afraid, my child, I'm with you."

She awoke.

Dizzy with a pounding pain in her temples.

"Are you all right, my child?" asked the same soft, kind, voice. She can feel a warm, firm hand on her forehead.

"She'll be okay," a man's voice said.

Ning-ning opened her eyes, slowly.

She saw two faces—a man and a woman—gazing at her. The man was a Westerner wearing round glasses. The woman was Chinese, young, beautiful and kind. Ning-ning's eyes opened wide. The woman looked like a nurse. Both she and the man were dressed in white.

"Yes, you'll be fine." The man's voice reassured, sounding as pleasant as Papa used to. "Drink something warm and you'll be much better. I'll be back later to have another look at you." He then turned and was gone.

"What's your name?" asked the nurse, kindly.

"Ning-ning." she mumbled, barely audible.

"Did you hear what Dr. Wilson said? Here. I've got some nice congee for you."

She got half a spoonful of congee, blew at it gently to make sure it was not too hot, and brought it to Ning-ning's lips.

Ning-ning opened her mouth, closed it around the spoon cautiously, and took in the congee. It tasted warm, soft, salty, and was so delicious. She let it swirl around in her mouth slowly, and swallowed, just like a baby.

The nurse gave her another spoonful, and Ning-ning took it eagerly. She felt hungry now, so hungry that she could finish the whole bowl in no time.

"Slowly! Slowly!" The nurse laughed.

Ning-ning allowed herself to smile.

"Where am I?" she asked.

"In the hospital," the nurse said.

"How did I get here?"

"Someone found you lying in the snow near Ninghai Road

last night."

"Who found me?"

"A German man. His name is John. John Rabe. I've seen him here before. He drove you here in his car."

"Why can't I remember?"

"You were unconscious, my child. Asleep." After a pause, the nurse said,

"You were talking about your Papa, Mama, and Grandpa."

"I dreamt it all?" Ning-ning said. The tears flowed down her cheeks once more.

"But you're alive." The nurse said.

"I'm all alone now!" Ning-ning sobbed.

"No, you're not alone. Look around! We're all here together." The nurse said. "See that young woman?" She whispered, pointing at the bed right next to Ning-ning's.

Ning-ning turned her head to look, and nodded.

The woman's face was wrapped in thick bandages. Underneath, her purple, swollen nose could be seen.

"When they found her, she was almost dead," the nurse whispered again.

"What happened?"

"The Red Cross folks saw her last night. Who knows where she came from? They found her at an old warehouse. Everyone thought she was dead, but then someone put their hand to her mouth and felt a faint breath."

The nurse stood up, turned to the woman's bed, bent closer to her face, and listened. She came back and sat down at Ning-ning's bed again.

"Is she okay?" Ning-ning asked.

"She'll make it."

"She had many stab wounds, her hands, her arms, her legs, just about everywhere. But her baby..."

"Her baby?" Ning-ning exclaimed,

"I'm sorry," said the nurse, "I didn't mean to upset you. But like you, she is a real fighter and Dr. Wilson said she will pull through."

"Can I eat by myself?" she asked the nurse, "so that you can help her and other patients?"

"Are you sure?"

She nodded.

The nurse helped Ning-ning sit up and went to the bed next to hers. Ning-ning turned her gaze outside the window.

It had stopped snowing. Ning-ning wasn't sure if it was early morning or late afternoon, but outside everything was white, veiled by a layer of glistening snow which hugged the ground and hung on every tree. She could picture the whole city—all of its trees, buildings, streets, ancient walls, the hills and mountains in the vicinities, even the majestic Purple Mountain—all being veiled by a layer of pure, white, glistening snow.

My hometown.

My hometown.

A commotion came from somewhere outside her ward, in the hall.

Heavy boots thumped on stairs. Hoarse voices shouted unintelligibly.

She froze for a moment, turning to look at the nurse, who was checking the young woman wrapped in bandages next to her.

"Monsters!" the nurse muttered through her teeth. She straightened up, stared at the door for a few seconds, and went back to work.

There is no safe place in my hometown now, Ning-ning thought. Not even in a hospital. But I am not alone. I will be okay.

Epilogue

The reign of terror, which began from the day the six divisions of the Imperial Army of Japan entered Nanking on December 13, 1937, continued well into the spring of 1938.

During those horrific weeks, hundreds of thousands of Chinese civilians and prisoners of war were murdered, and tens of thousands of women, including grandmothers and young girls, were raped, mutilated, or killed.

The city that sustained prolonged bombardment, shelling, arson, looting, and other unimaginable destructions lay in smoldering ruins for months.

Those horrific days also heralded unparalleled acts of humanity by a small group of foreigners who had chosen to remain within the Safety Zone even as the Japanese army closed in around them:

John Rabe, member of the Nazi party and chairman of the International Committee.

Robert Wilson, the only Western surgeon in the Safety Zone.

Minnie Vautrin, professor and acting dean of Ginling Arts and Science College for Women.

John Gillespie Magee, Episcopalian minister, chairman of the International Red Cross Committee of Nanking.

Miner Searle Bates, history professor at the University of Nanking, chairman of the International Committee after May 1939.

James Henry McCallum, member of the United Christian Missionary Society, a treasurer of the Safety Zone.

George A. Fitch, head of the YMCA in Nanking, an administrative director of the International Committee.

Ernest Forster, Episcopalian missionary, member of the International Committee.

Christian Kroger, German engineer, Nazi member of the International Committee.

Wilson P. Mills, Presbyterian missionary, member of the International Committee.

Lewis Strong Casey Smythe, secretary of the Intentional Committee.

The Safety Zone, an area of about two and a half square miles, has been credited with having accommodated and hence saved the lives of between 200,000-300,000 refugees, about half of all the people who were trapped within the walls when the Japanese entered the city.

The severity of the Japanese wartime atrocities committed in Nanking exacted an enormous toll on the members of the Safety Zone leadership.

George Fitch often suffered complete amnesia when delivering lectures on the subject in later years.

Sustained by his faith and love of China, Dr. Robert Wilson continued to operate on patients until he teetered on the brink of collapse. The long hours of relentless work led to a series of violent seizures as well as a complete mental breakdown from which he never fully recovered. He retuned to America in 1940.

That same year, Minnie Vautrin agreed to take a year's furlough and returned to America. Not long after her return, she ended her life by opening the gas jet of a kitchen stove.

John Rabe returned to Germany in April 1938, with his dairies and a copy of John Magee's film of the atrocities. Rather than gain an audience with Adolf Hitler, as he had hoped, Rabe was arrested and interrogated by the Gestapo. With the downfall of the Third Reich, Rabe was arrested by the Russians, then turned over to the British and forced to explain his connection to the Nazis. He lived in extreme poverty until he died from a stroke in 1950.

When news of the plight of John Rabe reached the people of Nanking in 1948, a year in which the civil war in China reached its most difficult stage, a fundraising campaign was begun and he was given the sum approximately equivalent to 2,000 American dollars at that time. The mayor of Nanking traveled to Germany to deliver in person, on behalf of the people of Nanking, money and a generous supply of food and provisions. They sent Rabe and his family a bundle of food each month until 1950.

The people of Nanking cherished a love for Minnie Vautrin which bordered on reverence, On her tombstone is engraved the following Chinese characters:

Gin Ling Yong Shen
("Ginling Forever")

Her epitaph reads:

Minnie Vautrin
Goddess of Mercy
Missionary to China
28 years
1886-1941

Today, The Nanking Massacre Memorial Hall stands on a former mass grave not far from Water West Gate, where some 8,000 bodies were exhumed. A series of galleries and walkways hewn from rough granite blocks, surrounded by solemn beds of stone, and precious living trees planted by Chinese and Japanese alike, served as a reminder that such human tragedy should never be forgotten. Nor repeated.

A Note on Chinese Names

Since *When The Purple Mountain Burns* is a historical novel, I generally follow the traditional Wade-Giles romanization system for historical Chinese figures such as Sun Yat-sen and Chiang Kai-shek. Otherwise, the pinyin system is used. Names of mountains, lakes and city gates are generally translated to better capture and reflect their connotative richness.

Acknowledgements

I am deeply indebted to the many scholars, journalists, survivors, and others whose courage, conviction, and humanity have inspired me and shaped this book profoundly.

Of the numerous sources for the book I am particularly indebted to the following: Timothy Brook's *Documents On The Rape Of Nanking*; Iris Chang's *The Rape Of Nanking: The Forgotten Holocaust Of World War II*; Joshua A. Fogel's *The Nanjing Massacre In History And Historiography*; Gao Anning's *Natural Conditions And Social Customs Of Qinhuai River*; Honda Katsuichi's *The Nanjing Massacre: A Japanese Journalist Confronts Japan's National Shame*; Hua-ling Hu's *American Goddess At The Rape Of Nanking: The Courage Of Minnie Vautrin*; Inazo Nitobe's *Bushido: The Warrior's Code*; Masahiro Yamamoto's *Nanking: Anatomy of An Atrocity*; Margaret Stetz and Bonnie B. C. Oh's *Legacies Of The Comfort Women Of World War II*; John E. Woods' *The Good Man Of Nanking: The Diaries Of John Rabe*; Yu Hua's *Sights Of Qin Huai River*; Zhang Kaiyuan's *Eyewitnesses To Massacre: American Missionaries Bear Witness To Japanese Atrocities In Nanjing*; and Zhu Chenshan's *The Picture Collection Of Nanjing Massacre And International Rescue*.

I would like to thank the staff at the Special Collections of Yale University Divinity School Library and the Hass Library of Western Connecticut State University for their cheerful technical assistance.

Heart-felt thanks go to numerous friends and colleagues who helped and inspired me in various ways, among them:

— Oscar De Los Santos for plowing through the complete manuscript and offering countless sensitive, insightful criticism;

— Fellow participants of the "Finishing Your Novel" workshop at the Peter Murphy Winter Poetry and Prose Getaway (January 16-19, 2004) for the rigorous, nurturing sessions, and for giving me a fresh pair of eyes to see my own writing;

— Louisa Burns-Bisogno for her extensive and enlightening comments on the screenplay based on this book; and

—Jimmy Cummings and Dorothy Aufiero for their passionate belief in both the novel and the screenplay.

I am deeply grateful to Chris Robyn at Long River Press for his intelligent and thoughtful guidance all the way through.

Finally, I owe so much to my father and mother for their love, and to Xiaohong, my wife, and Frank, my son, for their loving support.